About the book

Liv Scirocco has s hurl her back home in the middle of the night and to the protection of her sisters. She must focus on creating a better life this time, but the only man she's ever loved, the father of her deceased child, has returned and she can't avoid him. She wants to, though, because being near Hudson could mean her final unraveling.

Hudson Lozado's recent health scare made him question his life choices. He returns to his childhood beach town where the ocean can help him heal and find new direction. Instead, he found the woman who blames him for their son's death. The only woman he's ever loved.

But soul mates won't be denied, and Liv and Hudson realize that only a lie can destroy their connection. The baby they thought died at birth fifteen years ago might not be dead after all. Now two damaged souls will need to trust they have the strength to bring their worst nightmare to light and discover the truth or drown in the dark undercurrent of tragedy.

LIGHT UPON THE DARKNESS

STACEY WILK

Light Upon the Darkness

Copyright © 2021, Stacey Wilk

This book is dedicated to the members of
Stacey's Novel Family
*Thank you for being my constant readers. You do me a
tremendous honor when you read my books. I would always
be a writer, but you made me an author.*

CHAPTER 1

*H*e wanted to stand in the ocean because the salt-water waves were the only thing left to soothe his soul. Hudson Lozado parked his sedan in a diagonal spot in front of the boardwalk in Water Course and turned off the engine. The sun hadn't crested the horizon yet, leaving the sky in muted blacks and dark grays. He was always an early riser and couldn't stay another second in the stuffy apartment he had rented. So, he hopped on the Garden State Parkway over an hour ago to come home.

He had worked his ass off most of his life, and all he had to show for it were the suitcases in the trunk and the surfboard on the roof. The surfboard was a new edition. He hadn't surfed in fifteen years. Surfing was part of his life before. Before he lost it all the first time.

A first time existed because he lost it all again recently.

He pushed out of the car into the cold January morning. The wind whipped in from the water and coated him and the car with a light spray from the ocean. He grabbed his coat from the back and stepped onto the boardwalk. The old weather-worn boards creaked under his feet. The ocean rumbled its good morning with rough waves crashing against the sand. He forgot to buy a wetsuit. No winter ocean for him until he did.

As the sun climbed over the horizon, bringing with it the glow of golds and oranges the black sky began to fade away to make room for the new day. A few surfers in their full suits carried boards to the water and entered the ocean near the jetties. He was never a great surfer even though he had grown up at the beach.

His recent heart attack inspired him to revisit his old past-time. Life was too short he had learned at only thirty-six. He wanted to do only things he enjoyed, which meant quitting his job. He had donated all his suits too. He never wanted to wear a tie again.

He might've kept his job if his boss hadn't pissed him off. He had quit before he knew what he was saying. Now he had no job, no home, and a divorce under his belt. He was swinging for the fences.

The surfers waited patiently on their boards for the best wave to bring them in. Great surfers possessed the right amount of patience. He turned away with a small amount of regret and returned to his car. For the next several weeks, he planned on staying in his childhood house, spend as much time outside as possible, and relearn how to surf. After that, he wasn't sure. The idea that he had no plan for his future ignited a wild streak in him and made his palms sweat at the same time.

He navigated the narrow streets of town on his way to Cedar Street and stopped in front of his family's old Victorian. "What the hell?"

A blue and white realtor sign littered the front lawn. The words *under contract* at the top had him wondering if he was seeing straight.

He pulled into the driveway and hopped out of the car. He approached the sign as if it might bite him. He rocked the sign with his finger. It creaked on its hinges. His father hadn't said one stinking word about selling the house.

He dug his phone out of his pocket and pulled up his father's number. The phone rang and rang. Just as he expected the voicemail to answer, his father picked up.

"Hello?" The voice he would recognize anywhere barked over the line.

"You didn't tell me the house was for sale." He didn't see the point in easing into the conversation. His father had some questions to answer.

"Hudson? Is that you?"

"Yes, Dad. It's me." He let out a long breath. "Why didn't you mention you were selling our home?"

"Why would I say anything to you? It's my house."

He scratched at the beard he had grown in since the heart attack. Before then, his job always required he keep a clean shave. "I tried to understand when you wouldn't fly up from Florida to see me in the hospital, but why wouldn't you tell me you decided to sell our home?"

"It's just a house, and you haven't lived there in some time. How did you know about the sale anyway?"

"I'm standing on the front lawn."

"Why are you there?"

"Because I wanted to come home." He wouldn't bother to go into how his recent reality check had him worried about his mortality, or how he really had nowhere else to go. And worse, he would never mention that when he was home, he felt closer to *her*.

"I'm closing in a week, but you can stay there if you want. The place is basically empty except for the junk in the attic. I have a garbage company coming to take everything up there away."

"Everything? Even Mom's stuff?" After his mother had died, his father had shoved most of his mother's belongings into the attic. She had barely been in the ground before all signs of her had been erased.

"You were always too sensitive. Just like her."

He ignored his father's dig. He had spent his entire

4

life trying to be the kind of man his father had expected him to be, but often failed. If his father could see his beard and the length of his hair, he would cluck his tongue in disapproval. Wait until he found out that his only son quit his job and had purchased a surfboard.

"I want to go through whatever is up there." He had to make sure his father wasn't accidentally throwing away something valuable since he hadn't bothered to mark anything in the boxes when he packed Mom up.

If he were ever to have a child again, he would want his son or daughter to possess some of his mother's things. She had been so excited at the prospect of becoming a grandparent, and just as devastated as he was when things didn't work out.

"Why would you want to waste your time by going through old boxes?" His father's gravel-filled voice brought him back to the front lawn.

"Because Mom deserves to be more than yesterday's trash."

"The items in the boxes are all garbage, but suit yourself. I'll be up at the end of the week for the closing. Good bye, Hudson."

"See ya." He ended the call.

He had one week to make his way through the attic and collect old memories. Where would he go after that? He had no place to live, but he wouldn't leave until he had opened every box in the attic. The new owners would just have to deal with him even if it meant dragging every box outside onto the lawn and looking through them there.

He hadn't asked his father, the man with ice water in his veins, why he picked now to sell the house. He stared at the house and then the surfboard as if they would have an answer for him. There didn't have to be a good reason for his father's decision. He had decided to sell and that was that. Dr. Lozado's son didn't factor into any part of it.

He grabbed his bags from the trunk. He might as well get started. He let himself in through the back. The back door opened to a staircase that led to the upstairs apartment. His father had designed it as a way for the family to come and go without having to go through the office and interact with patients.

This old house wouldn't be in his family anymore. He had grown up here. He had brought only one woman to this home to meet his parents. That woman would be glad to see this house become something other than the space for his father's medical practice. He wished he could tell her about the sale. Maybe if the right person in town found out, she or he would tell her.

While he had lain in that hospital bed after the heart attack, he had missed her—Liv—so much he had dialed her number several times but never hit the send button. She would not come to him. She had made that clear when she had left and chose a life without him. That moment had been so long ago, and yet it burned his soul like it was yesterday. He would never get over her.

The stairs groaned under his weight, no happier to greet him than his father was. The inside of the house was almost as cold as it was outside. He flipped on the light in the kitchen.

He dropped his bags on the floor. The thud echoed in the empty space. He wandered from room to room. His father hadn't exaggerated. Nothing was here except a single roll of toilet paper in the hallway bathroom.

"How the hell am I going to stay in this place?" He scratched at his beard again.

He searched all the closets and found a set of sheets and a blanket shoved to the back of a high shelf. He adjusted the thermostat for more heat and the pipes shook and rattled in response. He would have to run to the general store and get some things for the next week like an air mattress and a folding chair. There wasn't even Wi-Fi available.

He went to the window that faced the ocean and threw it open to suck in the salt air. He paused until the gentle sound of the ocean met him.

Where was Liv right now? Probably taking photos of models in crazy outfits and barking out orders to anyone who wouldn't listen to her. He smiled in spite of the ache thoughts of Liv always caused. He had only wanted her to be happy even if that didn't include him. She was the mother of his son. The son who hadn't lived long enough to let his young, dumb dad hold him. If only he'd forced his father to let them hold the baby, maybe then he would've been able to forget about Liv.

He needed to keep his head about him right now. After he went through the attic, he would need to find a job and a direction. Emotions only muddied the waters. His father had been right about that much.

Tonight, he would start to tackle the attic. Tomorrow he'd go to the cemetery. At the end of the week, he would move on. At least in the meantime, he wouldn't bump into Liv around any corner and mess up his chance to get on with his life.

CHAPTER 2

The darkness was a girl's best friend. Liv Scirocco stumbled off the train at the Water Course station. The small stone building that sold tickets was deserted this time of night. Even the commuter lot was void of cars except for the solitary one parked under the light.

Winter made a shore town more of a ghost town. She huddled deeper into her coat, adjusted her duffel bag on her shoulder, and began the walk to her sister's house. Liv's relationship with winter wasn't much better than her relationship with men. The shore was meant for the long vibrant days of summer and not the fierce, cold winter wind that whipped off the ocean and snapped at her exposed skin as if it were an angry German shepherd.

No one knew she was coming. She hadn't bothered

to call first. She hadn't even bothered to change out of her tulle skirt before throwing her belongings into her bag and running for the train. Every time she swayed, the sickening sweet smell of raspberry sorbet and gin drifted under her nose. She tried to tug her coat over the spill stains, but the wool bounced back in defiance.

"Tonight was not one of your finer moments," she mumbled to herself as she made her way through town.

She didn't have the money for a driving service, and hadn't wanted to ask anyone to pick her up. But she had to get out of her crappy apartment. In the morning, her landlord would pack up her things and change the locks. Joke was on him. Everything she owned was in the duffel. The most important item being her camera.

The streets were narrow. Dirt-covered snow, plowed to make room for parked cars, spilled onto the sidewalks in spots like frozen cotton balls. She had to walk in the street a few times to avoid the snow.

She also avoided Cedar Street on her way to Mack's. She could go entire visits home without ever stepping near that road. Too many bad memories lay in wait like a stalker hoping to catch her off guard. But that didn't mean she didn't think about *him*. Hudson was woven into every thought. She only wished she could stop her mind's torturous wandering but had never figured out how.

Mack's adorable bungalow came into view. The white clapboards would glisten against the sunrise in a few hours. The light-blue shutters and flower boxes, empty now, gave the house a sweet, homey vibe. The waves crashed on the shore in a peaceful lullaby. If her life had been different, she could've seen herself in a house much like this one, filled with family and love. That had been the dream once.

A beat-up pickup truck sat in front of the house. She let out a long breath. Phoenix was at home. Phoenix loved her sister and her nephews, who would also be asleep now. He held a good position with the town fire department and owned a construction business with his brother Hawk, but she didn't understand why Mack liked that rough side of him that reminded her of sandpaper on skin.

She should've called first. What was she thinking showing up at her sister's house so late and disturbing them? They were a happy family and didn't need her problems. Phoenix was still mad at her, anyway. She had caused a scene at their summer party, another one of her less than finer moments. She had been jealous of her sister, not because she didn't want Mack to be happy. All she wanted was for her sisters to have a good life. But watching Phoenix with her nephews, loving them and taking care of them even though they weren't his, had only made her heart cry out for the baby she and Hud had lost.

No matter how much time went by, the pain didn't go away.

She turned on her heel and marched away. At the corner, she stopped. Tears threatened to spill. She swatted at her face. She had nowhere else to go. She had no job, no place to live, and was just about out of money.

With her broken pride, she forced herself up the front walk and rang the bell. The front rooms remained dark. Maybe no one heard. She dug her phone out of her pocket to send a text to Mack.

The porch light came on, and the door swung open. Phoenix glared at her in his white t-shirt and sweat pants. His hair stuck up in varying directions, and his jaw was dusted with beard growth. "What are you doing here?"

"Hey. I'm...I..." Her lip trembled. She tried to gulp down air to stop herself from breaking down.

"Are you drunk?" He narrowed his eyes.

She could only manage to shake her head. She had been drinking tonight at her friend's party, but any effects of the alcohol were long gone. She had sobered up pretty quickly when she went and dumped a full punch bowl on her ex.

"Phoenix, who is it?" Mack's voice whispered from somewhere inside the house.

She let out a long breath. She needed her sister. Phoenix held the door open wider.

"Mack." That one word was all it took. The tears spilled uncontrollably. She covered her face with her hands and broke.

Mack gathered her in her arms. She held on as if Mack were a rescue buoy.

"What did she do this time?" Phoenix said.

"Babe, shut up. Go back to bed." Mack led her inside and closed the door.

"Why do you hate me so much?" she said to Phoenix.

"I don't hate you, Liv. But I don't like what you have been doing to your sisters. Everyone has had a tough life. At some point you're going to have to deal with it." He ran a hand through his hair.

"Is that what you said to your brother when he screwed up his life?" She shouldn't bring Hawk into this. Their brother Wyatt had died when Hawk went off the rails. What she said wasn't nice, and it wasn't fair. Hawk had pulled his act together and won Aria back.

"You're damn right I did. Good night." Phoenix threw his hands in the air, but he went down the hall.

"Sit." Mack grabbed tissues and handed them to her. "Do you want some tea?"

She plopped onto the couch and blew her nose. "No, thank you." She squared her shoulders. "I need help."

"I can see that." Mack sat beside her. "What happened?"

"I lost my job." Her hands shook. She wasn't sure she could get through the whole story without a drink. The words tangled around her tongue and stuck to the roof of her mouth. Mack would think the worst of her when she found out what had happened.

"Can we skip to the part where you tell me everything? It's late, and I have to be up early for work." Mack gathered the blanket on the back of the couch and covered both of them.

"That is everything." She shrugged out of her coat.

"Livvie, it's me. We both know that's not the whole story. Start with why you lost your job. You needed it."

"Do you have anything stronger than tea?" She whispered in case Phoenix had bionic hearing. He would disapprove of her wanting anything to drink.

"Is that really a good idea right now? I can smell the booze on you from here."

She glanced under the blanket at her dress. "Why do you always think I drank too much? I spilled punch on myself."

Mack stood. "Look, if you don't want to talk about it, that's fine. You can sleep on the couch tonight, but without the whole story, you'll have to stay somewhere else. You can't stay here after last time. And I can't help you if you don't tell me everything."

Last time meant the summer house party to celebrate the renovations of Mack's bungalow. She had drunk too much and said terrible things about her sisters to a house full of people. She hadn't meant any of it.

"I'm sorry. Please sit with me." She pointed to the spot Mack had vacated. With a long breath, Mack sat. "I did spill punch on me when I dumped it on Darius's head."

"What?" Mack laughed.

"He showed up at Betsy's party with his pregnant girlfriend." She had already been a few drinks in by the time she grabbed that bowl. "He pulled me aside and said he meant to tell me, but he didn't think I would care since we had been broken up for months now. He said she wanted a baby so badly because she had miscarried before. When I got upset, he questioned why I was angry because I had no idea what it was like to lose a child. That's when I dumped the punch."

"Oh, I'm so sorry."

"He doesn't know about what happened to me, but his words hurt because I actually thought for a second maybe he and I could try to have a family. But that was right before I found out he was cheating on me with her."

"Is that what had you coming here in the middle of the night? A call or a text maybe, but you packed your stuff and hopped a train."

She might as well come clean. "Do you remember

those baby pictures of celebrities my boss made me take?"

She had been a top photographer for *Fluent Magazine* for years until her original boss quit. The new guy had said her work had lost all its heart, and she was washed up. He had assigned her the task of photographing the babies of celebrities.

"Sure. You hated the idea and let him know just how much."

"Well, right before Christmas I went to the hospital to take some photos. Some A-list actress had a baby. I always stop by the nursery on my way out to watch the newborns." The tears threatened to come again. She sat on her hands to stop them from shaking.

"There was a baby boy just crying and crying. None of the nurses were in there. I wasn't going to actually do it, but it was the holidays, and the anniversary is coming. My heart hurt and that little baby was crying…" The tears strangled her words.

"Livvie, what did you do?"

"I only went inside the nursery and picked him up." She hiccupped in between sobs. "I wanted to make him feel safe. I held him and spoke to him in a soft voice. I couldn't stop myself. He was so little and vulnerable. He needed someone to hold him." She wiped the tears from her face. "That was it. I swear. Then a nurse came in and called security. My boss fired me."

"Why did you pick up a baby in a hospital nursery?

Of course, someone would think you were trying to steal him."

"I don't know. I was stupid. But this last year, since the fire here, and I almost lost you and the boys, everything has disintegrated."

"Maybe it's time to start dealing with the past. It's been long enough."

"I keep thinking if Dr. Lozado had only let us hold our baby, maybe I could have moved on. Why didn't he let us hold him?" She had never been able to figure out why Hud's dad had said they couldn't see their boy. Hud had fought with him about it, but Dr. L had stood fast. She had been so out of it, she barely managed to breathe those first months.

"He must've thought it was best for some reason. But, Livvie, it's been fifteen years. You need to find a way through this." Mack grabbed her knee.

She jumped up as if Mack's touch had burned her. "Are you seriously going to tell me that if you lost Ian and Elliot you would ever get over it? You were going crazy over the possibility of losing custody. Do you think it matters that my son died at birth? Do you think I love him any less than you love yours? Tell me, Mack. I want to know."

Mack stood and faced her. "You need to calm down. You're yelling."

"Don't tell me to calm down. It was a mistake coming here." She scooped up her coat and bag.

Mack grabbed her arm. "Don't go. I'm sorry. I shouldn't have said what I did. I can't imagine what you feel. And you're right. I would die if anything happened to my boys. I just want you to be happy. You've suffered long enough."

"Thanks. I want happiness too." Maybe someday soon. She had been doing well for a while. She could even go full days without remembering the hurt. But when she and Mack and the boys had been trapped in this very house while it was on fire, fear had taken hold of her and had shaken free all she had created to keep the pain in the past.

"Can I stay here for a little while? I can sleep on the couch. I promise to play nice with Phoenix too."

Mack smiled and shook her head. "Give him a break, will you? He's a good man."

"Yeah, I know. He's Mr. Perfect."

"Let's not go that far. He leaves a mess everywhere. But he is pretty great, and I want you two to get along." Mack's face lit up. If she had her camera at the ready, she would've snapped the love, radiating off her sister.

"Okay. I'll do my best. Thank you." She hugged Mack one more time.

"I'm going to bed. Help yourself to whatever you want." Mack hugged her back and left her alone.

She flopped on the sofa and kicked off her shoes. Her mind wanted to run over the memories of Hud and the way he could make her laugh, because she once smiled the way Mack just had. But she forced those thoughts back into her memory box. Their time together was ancient history. He had moved on just like she had wanted him to. He had found a girl to marry, had a great job in the city, and last she heard living in a big house, making tons of money. He probably never gave her a second thought. She had been his biggest mistake. He had said as much.

She doubted she'd get much sleep, but she curled up on the couch and dragged the blanket over her. She needed something to distract her before she did make a big mistake and called Hud. She grabbed her phone out of her pocket and stared at the screen.

"Where are you, Hudson?" she said to herself. "Probably making love to his wife." She groaned. She needed to move on the way Hud had. She wondered if he ever thought about her and their baby. Did he remember the anniversary of that night the way she did?

She dialed another number. The only other number she would call at this hour.

"Livvie? Is that you?" Blair yelled into the phone. People laughing and carrying on, along with loud music and the clanking of silverware played like an orchestra in the background.

"Yeah. Where are you?" She raised her voice too.

"I'm out with friends. Where are you?"

"In Water Course. At Mack's." She plucked at the fuzz on the blanket.

"What are you doing there?" Blair's tone was a dash of disdain mixed with a dose of confusion. She would do anything to avoid their hometown. Blair hadn't been home in several years.

"I had some problems at work. And I got evicted." Sometimes talking with Blair was easier than speaking with her other sisters because Aria and Mack had their lives together in a way she and Blair hadn't captured.

"What? I'm having trouble hearing you. It's so loud in here. Can I call you tomorrow? No, wait. How about the day after? Can I call you then?"

"Sure." Her heart sank.

"Thanks, you're the best. Bye." Blair ended the call.

She threw back the blanket and went in search of something to drink. Mack had said to help herself to whatever she wanted. Well, she wanted some company. She found a bottle of pinot noir already chilled in the fridge. She grabbed a glass and her coat and went onto the porch.

A cold, biting wind whipped in off the ocean and shook her. She'd have only one glass, and she would buy her sister a new bottle tomorrow. After tonight she would stop. Or Phoenix would be right.

But she wasn't sabotaging her own life. Life just hadn't been fair.

Ever.

CHAPTER 3

"*A*unt Livvie, wake up." A six-year-old Ian planted a wet kiss on her cheek.

Liv blinked against the adorable assault and the morning sun streaming through the windows.

Ian shook her with his chubby fist then wrapped her in a milk-crusted hug. She lifted her head off the sofa, but the pain slammed it back down. Her mouth tasted like the bottom of a shoe dragged through mud. She needed strong coffee and a hot shower before being greeted by her sweet-smelling nephew.

"Hey, buddy." Her voice scraped across her throat. She had drunk too much even after she swore to herself, she would stop at one glass. She had only wanted to rest her eyes before chugging some water and brushing her teeth. She hadn't meant to spend the rest of the night sleeping in her clothes and, worse, her bra.

"I had to wait to wake you up. Phoenix said we should let you sleep. Do you want to take us to school today? I'm going to bring home the class ferret next week. Do you want to see a picture of it?" He bounced on his toes, with a wide missing-tooth smile.

"Would it be okay if I had some breakfast before I answer all those questions?" She tossed the blanket aside and swung her legs off the couch. Her head spun in the sudden rush of movement. She held her breath for a second before trying out her wobbly legs.

"Ian, pal, can you put your shoes on? We need to leave for school." Phoenix sauntered into the living room in his gray wool crew neck and black faded khakis. His hair was smoothed in place compared to last night's slept-in look.

"I'll be right back." Ian ran from the room.

"Were you drinking last night?" Phoenix held up the empty wine bottle.

"I bought it empty. Go away." She should've booked a room at the B and B, then Phoenix couldn't judge her.

"Mack asked me to help you out today. Get dressed. The boys and I will wait in the truck for you."

"Where is Mack?" She ran her hands through her hair and tried to create a little saliva in her mouth.

"She goes to work earlier when I don't have a

morning shift." Phoenix dumped the bottle in the recycling bin in the drawer.

"Tell Mack thanks, I don't need any more help. She's done enough just by letting me stay here. Besides, I have plans." She had no plans of any kind. She should probably start looking for a job. Maybe the florist was hiring, or she could be a greeter at the warehouse store out on the highway.

"I can't believe I'm saying this. I have a possible job for you. But if you're going to continue to drink until you pass out, I'm not so sure giving you a job or letting you stay near Ian and Elliot is a good idea." He fisted his hands on his narrow hips.

"I would never do anything to hurt those boys." She located a glass and pressed some buttons on the fridge door to make water appear. The cold water relieved some of the yuck in her mouth.

She would give her life for those kids, and had practically done it last winter when Mack's crazy ex-husband locked them all in the house and set it on fire.

"I actually believe that. Now please, do whatever it is you do in the morning so we can get out of here. I don't want the boys to be late." He grabbed his coat off the hook by the door. "Ian, Elliott, let's go."

The pounding of small feet echoed into the room followed by Ian in his red coat unzipped and floating behind him. Elliott entered second with his blue coat zipped up to his neck. His backpack was firmly in its rightful place while Ian's was open and dropping stuff behind him. Her heart squeezed. Staying here this time might be a mistake since her stupid move at the hospital. Holding that baby had been the last unravelling after a year of frayed moments.

"Hello, Aunt Liv," Elliott said.

"Hey, kiddo. Can I get a hug?" She held her arms out, and she didn't lose her balance. Score one for her.

Elliott walked over and stuck out his hand. "Is it okay if we shake hands?" His brows were drawn together. He was so much like his biological father. She was glad the boys, but especially Elliott, had Phoenix now. He would help Elliott not take life so seriously.

She risked a quick glance at Phoenix. He shrugged and nodded.

"You got it." She gripped his little hand in hers before he returned to his spot by his brother. Ian patted Elliott on the head.

"Okay, you two, wait for me on the porch." Phoenix shrugged into his coat. "Now tell me, where are you waiting?"

"The porch," the boys said together.

"Where? I can't hear you." He put a hand to his ear.

"The porch," they yelled. Ian jumped up and down.

"Excellent, men. Fall out." Phoenix held the door open for the boys. He gave them one more reminder, then closed the door halfway.

"You are very good with them." She meant that.

Phoenix was a natural with her nephews. He had no children of his own and didn't seem in any hurry to have any. He wanted to adopt the boys since their biological father was a criminal and on the run. Mack had started the paperwork.

"Thanks. They're great." A red blush crossed his cheeks. "You have five minutes to meet us outside." He turned to go.

"What kind of a job do you have for me and why?" Her curiosity was piqued. Phoenix had a job for her. She hoped it wasn't mopping the floors of the firehouse, but if it were, she'd have to say yes with a smile. Beggars couldn't be choosers and all that. She would save up some cash and then move on to anywhere but here. Water Course was a nice place to visit, but to stay would require her to escape reality too often.

"Does it matter what the job is?" He turned back to her.

"Kind of. And why are you being so nice to me?" Not that his tone indicated niceness in any way, but she never expected Phoenix to offer her an employment opportunity.

"Mack asked me to make some calls this morning. You got lucky something came up.""Do you always do what she tells you to?" She limped over and turned on the coffee maker.

"Pretty much." He flashed a high-voltage smile, then dropped it so quickly she almost missed it. The smile was for Mack. The pursed lips were for her. "Skip the coffee and get dressed. The boys can't be late for school, and Mack wants me to bring you to the bakery."

"My big sis loves me." She turned the coffee maker back off. She had always missed Mack when they weren't together. Mack had a way of making her feel wanted. She could use more time with Mack even if she were covered in flour, racing around the bakery making her customers feel wanted too.

"I have no idea why." He shook his head with a grimace.

"Shut up, Phoenix."

"Make me," he teased.

"You're such a child."

"I'll be outside. Don't take too long." He left without another word.

She opened the recycle container and stuck her tongue out at the wine bottle. "I'm done with you."

She meant it this time.

"I'm not doing that." Liv cradled the coffee mug against her chest and let the warmth from the ceramic seep through her shirt. The caffeine cleared her head enough to make certain this idea was not happening.

Mack and Phoenix stared at her with wide eyes

from the other side of the bakery counter. Mack owned their grandfather's old bakery. Mack was the only Scirocco girl bitten by the baking bug. They were all glad to hand the store over to Mack and see her prosper with Pop's recipes. She had updated the store over the years and now offered a colorful display of cookies and pastries that had tourists coming for miles and year-rounders here every day.

The place buzzed with customers all around them like bees to a hive. Some sat deep in conversation at the few tables she offered. Two men in dirty sweatshirts, work boots, and jeans stood in the corner with coffee and talked about the high tide and the surfers. A woman tapped at her phone with red-lacquered nails while she poured a large amount of sugar into her cup.

"It's good money," Mack said, interrupting her thoughts.

"I don't want to take pictures of car accidents and burned-out houses. It's creepy." She hadn't expected the job offer to be working for the local insurance company taking pictures for accident reports. She would've rather mopped floors. "Can't I work here with you?"

"I can't afford any additional help this time of year. If it were summer, I could take you on, but in the winter, we just make ends meet."

"This place is full of customers." She pointed around the room.

"In an hour it will be dead, and probably for the rest of the day. Phoenix has put his neck out on the line for you."

"I didn't ask him to do that." She shot a glare at him. She had only been in town a few hours, but it seemed Mack and Phoenix didn't completely trust her.

He pushed off the counter and turned to Mack. "I'm going over to the station. Let me know if she changes her mind." He kissed Mack and sauntered out with a wave to the guy bringing bread out from the back.

"Don't be so obstinate, Livvie. You need a job, and there's one for you. Do you know how lucky that is in a town this size especially this time of year?" Mack restocked the napkin dispenser.

"But what if there are dead bodies?" She would pass out if she saw a dead body.

"You don't photograph the people. Just the items. You know, the cars, the inside of the houses after the fire chief says you can go in. You don't even have to do anything with the pictures afterward. You just send them. It's easy work. You just have to be on call. That means no drinking."

"He told you about this morning." She tried to hide behind the coffee mug.

"I asked him. Phoenix and I don't have secrets from each other. That's not how a relationship works."

Mack was referring to her and the big secret she had kept from every man she had ever been involved

28

with since Hudson. She couldn't bring herself to share what had happened. It was her story. Hers and Hud's. No one else was welcome into that memory.

"I'm not an alcoholic, Mack."

"I think you might need some help. Why not find a group or something you can join?" Mack waved the woman with the red nails as she left the store.

"I don't need that kind of help. I need a job. So, I guess you can call your boyfriend and tell him I accept. How will I get around? I don't have a car." She couldn't control the grumble in her voice, and wanted to kick herself for sounding ungrateful. She needed more caffeine.

Mack pulled keys from her pocket. "You can take mine for now. I don't go too many places besides home and the bakery. I can use Phoenix's truck or borrow Aria's car. We'll make it work."

"That's just great. Five adults sharing four cars." But she swiped the keys anyway. She had managed to pull up her boot straps after she lost the baby and make a life for herself. But in the matter of a year, she had fallen so far, she didn't know how she got there.

She gripped Mack's hand and squeezed. "Thank you. I should've said that first. Thank you for helping me out. I really do appreciate it." She did. If it hadn't been for her sisters, she would have nothing.

"I know you do. It's all going to work out. You'll see. Here is the information on the insurance company."

Mack handed over a red file folder with papers inside. "They have an office right off of Main Street. Milly Marshall is the office manager. She's expecting you."

"You did this all for me." She waved the folder in the air and fought back the tears on the edge of existence. She really needed to stop crying all the time.

"It's what family is for." Mack came around the counter and pulled her into a hug. She held on and inhaled Mack's cinnamon and sugar smell. "You were there for me last year when I needed help. Now it's my turn to return the favor."

She eased out of the embrace. "You're doing way more than I did. I just stayed with you for a few days."

"If you hadn't been there, I might've lost the boys. I don't know what I would've done if anything had happened to them. You helped us get out of that fire. All you need now is a fresh start. That's what I'm giving you. But please, Liv, don't screw this up. I won't be able to help you if you do. I have the boys and Phoenix to think about."

"I promise not to make a scene at any more of your parties." She gave Mack a half-smile.

Mack choked out a laugh. "Glad to hear it. I have to get back to work. I'll talk to you later." Mack gave her another quick hug and disappeared through the swinging doors into the back.

She pushed out into the cold air and pulled up the zipper of her jacket to her chin. The bakery wasn't far from this insurance office. She could walk, then come back later for Mack's car. She didn't want the car. She didn't want the job, but that she would take. If only to move on.

She had been glad to help Mack last year with the boys. Even when they were stuck in the house while it was on fire, she was grateful she had been there to climb out the window and get the boys to safety. She didn't want any of her sisters to know what it felt like to lose a child. Not even Blair, who still didn't have any kids of her own yet.

The door to the general store swung open. She stopped short not to get hit. She was about to blast the person for being in a rush and not looking, but her breath caught. A tall man with dark hair leaned his barn-coat wearing back against the door as if his hands were too full to use them. Time stopped. The street disappeared, taking every sound with it except the roaring in her ears. It couldn't be. Impossible.

He walked away with his back still to her, and the door swung shut with a thump. He had long legs clad in faded jeans, and his stride was fast and sure. Like him.

The words formed in her mouth, but her tongue twisted them into knots. What if he didn't want to see her? She had made it pretty clear the last time they spoke she didn't want him coming around anymore.

A car horn honked somewhere in the distance and

threw her out of her trance. What was he doing in town? Her feet hurried after him as if they knew better than her head, her footsteps echoing on the pavement. He stopped at a car and rummaged in his pants pocket, still unaware of her. It wasn't too late to turn and run.

He wasn't supposed to be here. He never came home. She had kept track of that. His absence from town was the reason Water Course was a safe place for her to visit and return to. She didn't risk bumping into him.

Her phone went off. The annoying, loud ring she always used so she wouldn't miss a call shattered the morning, betraying her.

He turned as if in slow motion. She begged her feet to move. Except it wasn't her feet that finally got the message straight.

"Hudson," she said.

CHAPTER 4

*H*udson blinked a few times because what he saw couldn't be right. Had the heart attack screwed with his neurological functions as well?

"Liv?" She stood before him as beautiful as ever. Her black hair flowed in long waves like the ocean around her face and down her shoulders. Her lips pressed in a thin line. Lips he had kissed a thousand times. But her eyes seemed haunted or maybe that was his own reflection coming back at him. He was haunted by her in his dreams. Even now.

She fidgeted with the belt on her coat. "It's so nice to see you. Your beard and your hair…it's a good look on you." She smiled and pointed, but she ducked her chin and hid her eyes.

He adjusted the box of items he had purchased to make his stay more comfortable. After sleeping on the

STACEY WILK

floor last night, the air mattress had become a necessity.

He never expected to see Liv standing on the sidewalk. Owen had assured him Liv rarely visited and when she did it was never more than a few days. The odds were in his favor he could go several weeks without laying eyes on her. So much for good odds.

He scratched at his jaw. "Thanks. Good to see you too. What brings you to town?" He wanted to drop the damn box, scoop her up in his arms, and swing her around, but he stayed put.

He wanted to know everything about her, not just the things he had read on the internet. Why was she there? How long would she stay? Where was she going? Had she allowed some other man into her heart?

"I'm visiting with Mack and Aria for a while. How about you?" She bunched her fingers in her curls, that thing she did when she was nervous. He would often take her hand and squeeze it when she did that. His Liv was still the same.

"My dad is selling the house. I'm cleaning out the attic." He lifted the box as if that explained everything. But he couldn't say more. He couldn't tell her how his life fell apart again or how his dad didn't want him in said attic which was probably code for he didn't want him in the house at all.

"He's finally selling that place." She turned her gaze away as if lost in a memory. When she looked

34

back at him, she pressed her lips into a thin line again and shrugged. "I heard you got married. Congratulations."

This conversation made his insides ache. The tension between them could power an engine. He didn't want to be some old classmate from high school she couldn't remember or barely tolerate, and yet her clipped voice and insipid eyes said he had become just that.

"We divorced two years ago. Are you still taking pictures?" He had laid his heart out to this very woman, bared his soul to her, and now standing on a cold winter sidewalk he was at a loss on how to reach her heart again. Hadn't that always been his problem?

"I just finished up a shoot recently. I should let you go. That box looks heavy."

"Where are you headed?" He didn't want her to go just yet. It had been too many years since he last spoke to her.

"Um. I have an appointment. It was good to see you, Hud. Take care." She ducked past him and marched down the sidewalk with her head high.

"Liv, wait."

She stopped but didn't turn. He held his breath, hoping for a sign that she felt some of the churning that he did. That she had missed him as much as he missed her, that maybe, just maybe she regretted what she had said.

She looked at him over her shoulder. "Don't do this." Her words were a whisper on the cold wind.

But he couldn't stop himself. His mouth raced on before she could run away. "After your appointment, do you want to get a drink? Just to catch up. We're both in town at the same time on the same street. That's some kind of coincidence. What do you say?"

"I say no, thank you." She turned on her heel and walked away.

He watched her until she turned the corner and out of sight. What was he thinking asking her out for drinks? She had made it perfectly clear she wanted nothing to do with him. He dumped the box into the truck and stole one more look in the direction she went. The street was as void as his gut. He headed home with nowhere else to go.

He kicked the back door into the kitchen closed because his hands were full, and he still seethed from Liv walking away from him. He dropped the box. The things he bought clanked against each other the way his thoughts banged around in his head. He needed to stop thinking about Liv. Hadn't enough time gone by? What else did he need from her?

He reached for a beer in the fridge. He had stocked up on groceries yesterday. Now it was time to go into the attic and sift through that junk to find anything of his mom's. His mother had loved this house. She had come from nothing. Her parents were Italian immigrants who had lived in an apartment over a garage their whole time in America. Owning this home had been a source of pride for her, being the first person in her family to own property. He would do anything for his mother and her memory.

He abandoned the beer. It was too early to start drinking and grabbed the air mattress from his collection of purchases from the general store. He had also bought a wet suit. His fingers ran over the neoprene material. Tomorrow morning, he would try his hand at a piece of a new life. Hopefully, he didn't make too much of an ass of himself out there.

His phone vibrated in his pocket. He let out a long sigh when he read the caller on the screen. "Hey, Dad. What's up?"

"Hudson, it's me."

"I know." His father never seemed to catch on to technology. He couldn't figure out if it was an act of defiance on his father's part because he hated technology or simple misunderstanding.

"Someone from the new owner's insurance company is coming over to take photos of the medical office. I need you to deal with them." Over the years, his father's accent grew heavier as if he didn't have the energy anymore to keep it hidden. He never understood why his father thought his words laced with a hint of Spanish was a bad thing.

"Why are they doing that? Can't it wait until you

close? It's only a week away." He should've expected something like this to happen. The minute his father knew he was in town, his dad would want him to take responsibility for the house.

"I didn't ask why, and I don't care why. Just let them in. It's not as if you're busy. You're on vacation over there."

"I'm recuperating from my heart attack. And I feel better today, thanks for asking." He wiped a hand over his face and scratched at his beard.

"You don't need much recuperating. You're young and in good health. That medicine you're taking will keep your blood thin. Something else will kill you before your heart will."

"Gee, thanks, Dad." His father's bedside manner was not his best doctoring skill. The patients had come to him because he could diagnose what was wrong with them and make them feel better without a lot of unnecessary tests. Most of them just ignored the bite in his words. And the old-timers had just bit him back.

"Please let the person in and stay with them while they take the pictures. I don't want them stealing anything."

"Dad, there isn't anything worth stealing." He shook his head. His father was losing his mind. His dad had always been a touch paranoid, worrying other people would judge him or want what he had acquired, but lately it seemed as if that was worse.

"Don't let this person go in the attic. Do you hear me?"

"What is it with you and that attic?"

"I had wanted it cleared out before anyone went up there. Someone could trip over that junk and get hurt. Then they would sue me. I can't have that."

"Okay, whatever you say. No attic." He hung up, unable to continue the conversation. He had tried to spend as little time with his father as possible after his mother died.

She had been the glue that held their family together. Without her, Hud didn't see much point in keeping up appearances. His father always had his head in his work where he wasn't required to show any emotion. Being a doctor had been a good choice for his dad. A doctor that didn't get emotionally involved with his patients was someone who could keep his sanity while keeping his patients healthy.

After he and Liv had lost their son, dealing with his father had been almost impossible. He had needed his dad to understand how much he was hurting, but his father had told him to move on because nothing could change it. Instead of being supportive, his father had rationalized and offered unwanted solutions.

What were the odds he would bump into Liv today? He certainly hadn't expected to find her standing only inches from him and stealing his breath right out of his lungs. Of course, he hadn't planned on going into town while he was here. Now the house seemed to have decided for him.

He made a cup of coffee. The coffee would help keep him warm while he went through some of the boxes. He glanced at his laptop. A quick search would only take five minutes. The day stretched out before him. He still had plenty of time to dig through the junk in the attic.

Grabbing his laptop off the counter, he opened the search engine. He had searched her many times before. His ex-wife had caught him once. When she had asked who Liv was, he had refused to tell. He had never shared what had happened to them. It was their story and their story alone. He wouldn't betray Liv's privacy by telling her pain to another person. She would have hated for a stranger to know her business. Keeping her secrets was the least he could do for her.

The doorbell rang as he clicked through some of the sites that talked about her work. He reluctantly pushed away from the computer and went downstairs and through the foyer that had doubled as the patient waiting area. He opened the door, and his heart nearly stopped for a second time in his life.

Liv brushed past him. "Don't say a thing."

CHAPTER 5

Why did he have to look so damn good?

Liv fidgeted with her camera hanging around her neck. Standing in Dr. Lozado's office with the same green tapestry rug faded from the years made her hands sweat and the acid in her stomach burn. The furnishings were gone, but the place still had the same effect on her. It didn't matter that it had been years since she was here. The worst night of her life happened in this house. She forced herself not to think about it, or she would want a drink.

"You work for the insurance company?" Hud stared at her with eyes as wide as trash cans. He hadn't changed much in all these years. He had new lines around his eyes and dark circles where there had been none.

Through the years, she had avoided searching for him because she couldn't bear to see him happy with someone else even though she had been the one to end things. It had been a rash decision she had regretted, but she couldn't put her pride away long enough to beg him to take her back. She had blamed him for their misery at first, but it hadn't been his fault. It had all been hers.

"It appears that way." She held up the camera.

"I don't understand."

"Nothing to understand, Hud. I'm here to take pictures. Let's get this over with so I can leave you to whatever it is you were doing." Another quick glance around showed her the entire first floor was old and worn with chipped paint on the walls and yellowed blinds that leaked the sun through them like a cyst oozing.

The room on the other side of the foyer was the place she had lost her baby. Her knees buckled, but she righted herself before anything foolish could happen. Hud didn't notice. His face remained impassive. Same old Hud.

"Hang on a second. Is this some kind of a joke? Because honestly, I'm not in the mood for your games." He opened the door again and looked out. The cold wind swirled in on an angry burst.

"No one else is coming. Just me. This isn't a joke." She couldn't meet his intense gaze. Her humiliation could choke a horse. She hadn't wanted to come here when Milly had given her this assignment. She had asked the same thing about the joke. Milly hadn't found any humor in it.

She had stood on the front walk for five full minutes before she had mustered up the courage to ring the bell. If she hadn't needed the money so badly, she would've told Milly to shove this job. She also didn't want to embarrass Mack or Phoenix. They were helping her.

Hud wasn't the only reason she didn't want to come here. How could she face the place where she lost her baby? The last time she stood in this spot she was in labor and scared out of her mind. And when she had left this house the very last time, she was broken in a million pieces.

"Why are you taking pictures for an insurance company? Don't you have a job working for a fashion magazine?" He crossed his arms over his chest and cocked one brow in that way he did when he tried to size up a situation before he made a decision.

Hud wasn't much of a risk-taker. He had always wanted to know his odds first. Safe, sure, and reliable. Which didn't explain the surfboard leaning against the side of the house. He hadn't had much of an interest in surfing when his friend Owen had dragged him out to catch waves.

"What's up with the surfboard?" Better if she threw him off the scent of her failed career at the magazine.

He shoved his hands in his pockets. "The surfboard? Oh, you saw that?"

"It's right outside." Where she stood debating whether or not to ring the bell or run for her life.

"Yeah, well, I wanted to surf while I was in town. I missed it. How long are you back for?"

"I don't know. I was told to take photos of the downstairs." She didn't want the conversation on her. If she could just take the pictures and leave, this little meeting won't have to mean anything. She unscrewed the lens cap, but her shaking hands dropped it. The cap rolled away and landed at Hud's foot.

"Did you know about this little appointment when I bumped into you not an hour ago?" He retrieved the cap, but didn't hand it back.

"No." She wished she had known, then she could've either prepared him or herself.

"I don't believe you." He tapped the cap on his finger. The click of plastic on his skin made her heart race more.

"Well, believe it. The appointment I said I had was with the insurance company. Today is my first day. I'd really like to get to it, if you don't mind." She squared her shoulders and tilted her chin. She didn't need to explain herself to him, but she didn't like that he believed she was up to something. He had to know how hard being here was for her.

"Can I get you something to drink? I was just making coffee."

The last thing she needed was caffeine. Her heart raced as if it were swimming in coffee. "Hud, I don't want to socialize. I just want to do my job so I can get out of your father's office."

"I'm sorry. I didn't think. I should've—"

"Stop. I don't want to talk about it. I'll start in here." She would photograph the worst room first.

The space was only four walls and a floor. Everything was gone. The hospital bed she had climbed onto. The cabinets and counter filled with medical stuff. The monitor that Dr. L had hooked up to her belly. Taking photographs would last for five seconds, but her hands still shook. She could barely hold the camera. Her breath came in short bursts. Her vision blurred. She tried to inhale, but her lungs wouldn't cooperate.

Sweat broke out on her lip. She turned to find Hud. "I...I..." She gripped her throat.

He put an arm around her shoulders and walked her out of the room. "You're okay, Liv. I'm here."

He led her to the back room where the entrance to the family's quarters was. The room had also been used for supplies and a small kitchen for Dr. Lozado to use during the day. The distance between her and that room allowed her lungs to work again. She eased away from his touch.

Feeling his strength around her was almost as unbearable as facing that awful room, but for very different reasons.

"Thanks, I'm okay. I don't know what happened." That was a lie. She hadn't expected her reaction to be quite that acute. It was just a room.

"I understand. Maybe too much these days." He leaned against the wall. The color drained from his face. He held a hand over his eyes.

"Hey, are you okay?" It was her turn to help him. She would always worry about him, and right now he seemed about ready to fall over. They were quite a pair at the moment.

"I'm fine. Just like you."

She didn't believe him. He didn't look fine. He looked tired and worn out. Exactly the way she felt. But she doubted it was for the same reasons. "Can I get you that coffee?"

"I said I'm fine." He pushed off the wall and held her gaze. He could be as stubborn as he wanted. If he toppled over, so be it.

"You aren't going to tell me why you almost passed out?"

"The flu." He glanced away.

He lied. Whatever it was, he didn't want her to know. A million questions jumbled in her mind. Was he dying? She wanted to reach for him, but she didn't dare move.

"You didn't answer my question before. Why are you working for this insurance company and not taking your fancy photos?" The shift from him to her was his way to end the conversation. If that was how he wanted it, so be it. She wasn't going to force him to tell her his problems. He wasn't hers.

"Why do you think? Why would I give up my job in the city to take pictures for Milly Marshall?" She held his gaze. She would have to come to terms with the fact her life fell apart again or maybe still falling apart because she clearly was a mess.

But she wanted to blurt it all out right onto his broad shoulders. Hud could carry the weight of it all, and she had loved that about him. If he was sick, she would never burden him, and truthfully, she kept her lips closed because she didn't want him to think how lucky he was to have gotten away from her when he had been the one good thing in her life besides their child.

"Tell me what happened with your job." He handed back the lens cap.

"It's a long story." Now wasn't the time to tell him everything from the moment Darius dumped her to the day in the hospital when she held that baby in the nursery to her boss firing her.

She would save him the details. No matter how nice he was being to her, he couldn't want her here anymore than she wanted to be standing inches from him.

"Tell me." A small smile slipped over his lips, inviting her to trust him. She remembered how those lips tasted and the way they slid over her skin, making her beg him for more.

"I don't want to." She ran her fingers through her hair.

"You're a bad liar. You want to spill. Go ahead. Tell me."

"Absolutely not. You'll go running and tell Owen."

"Not a chance. Did you get arrested or something? Did you steal from your boss? You had a wild streak, but I'm pretty sure you weren't a criminal."

Being with him was like grabbing a favorite old and perfectly worn-in sweatshirt. He fit her and made her feel safe. "I should just take those photos and get out of your way."

"Let me."

"Excuse me?"

"Let me take the photos for you. I know why you got so upset out there. It would be hard for anyone to return to the place where the worst thing that had happened to them occurred. Even I couldn't go in there for years. Let me help you." He held out his hand.

"I can't let you do that."

"Why not? Hard can it be? I point and click."

"I don't need you to save me."

A darkness passed over his eyes. "Of course not. Not Liv Scirocco. She never needs anyone. She's got it all handled all by herself."

"Just like you."

"What?"

"Give me a break. You won't tell me what's going on with you, but you want me to tell you all my crap."

"You don't want to talk to me because you don't want to have the conversation we've never had. I just had a little cold. It's not worth talking about."

"There's no point in talking about the past anymore."

"Because you said so."

"Damn right because I said so. What do we have to say? We lost our son. End of story. You needed to get on with your life and so did I. That's it."

"That's not it. I never wanted us to break up. I wanted a say and you took that away from me."

"You don't get a say, Hud. Shocker. Being around you was too much to take. I needed the memory to fade away, and I couldn't do that with you hanging around."

"Did you manage to make the memory go away?"

"Yes."

"Liar."

His words were like a slap across the face. He could always see right through her. She shoved the lens cap into her pocket. "I have to take those pictures."

She didn't wait for him to say anything. She forced

49

her legs forward until she stood in the front room again. The end of day shadows had grown long in there now that the sun was behind the house and almost gone.

She hadn't meant to lose it in front of him. Protecting herself from the truth was impossible now that Hud had walked into her life and started up that old conversation.

She had been piling on the layers of denial for years. But ever since the fire last year, those layers had come loose. Holding that baby in the nursery was the last layer left over a hole so large if she fell in it, she could die from the grief.

Now, here, in Hud's house, with the smell of his woodsy scent clinging to her, she had to face her demons that lurked around every corner and had her running for her life.

She still loved him.

She wanted their son.

And she didn't want to be alone anymore.

"I DON'T BLAME you for what happened."

Liv turned to him with her camera still pointed at the inside of the room his father used to use as an office. This room was just as empty as all the others. The hardwood floor had a million scratches on it from the years of patients taking a seat opposite their doctor to hear about their health.

He had done much the same thing right before he hit the road to come to Water Course. He had sat opposite his cardiologist to hear what was in store for him now that he had thrombophilia.

"What did you say?" she said.

"I blame myself. It was my responsibility to take care of you and our son. I failed you both. I should've been there." His insides burned. They needed to have this conversation once and for all.

"You tried." She turned back to her work, dismissing him like always.

"Damn it. Don't turn away from me again. You can't keep avoiding me now, standing here in the place it happened. For once, for one damn time, talk to me so I can go on with my life." He wasn't supposed to get upset. He was still recuperating, but she needed to understand.

"You want to drag it all out and spread it around like a fungus? Fine. You're off the hook. No one blames you. Not the perfect Hudson Lozado with a bright future. Our son's death was my fault." She pounded her chest. "I should've been able to protect him. What kind of mother loses her son during delivery? It's the fucking twenty-first century. How could I have messed up that badly?" She threw her hands in the air.

Liv had a way of riling him up like no one else. He

wished she wouldn't point that doggedness directly at him, but she had spent a lifetime fighting for everything, and losing most of the time. He had always admired her tenacity. He still did.

"You've been blaming yourself this whole time?" He had believed he was the target of her anger.

"Who else would I blame?"

"Me. You wouldn't even look at me. I begged you to talk to me."

"Hud, I don't want to talk about this anymore. I'm exhausted. I barely slept last night and being here is killing me. I wouldn't even have come if I didn't need the job so badly. Can we just forget about it?"

"Forget about our son?" He leaned against the wall and rubbed the heels of his hands into his eyes. The pressure released some of the pain building behind them.

"Hud, you don't look good."

"Gee, thanks." He shook his head and almost laughed.

"I didn't mean it like that. I'm sorry I blew up at you." She stepped closer. "Is it more than the flu?" She placed her cool hand on his heated forehead. Her scent, something like black licorice and suede, seduced him. He pushed her hand away, or he might do something foolish like kiss her.

He didn't want her pity. She didn't need to know

about the unexpected heart attack that had blindsided him. He wouldn't tell her.

He had been fine one minute and then gasping for breath the next. The doctors said it was genetic. That all his workouts and eating right would never have stopped the attack. The diagnosis didn't make him feel any better.

"I'm fine. Answer me. Are you trying to forget about our son?" he said.

"No. That would be impossible." She let out a long breath. "I want to forget about being in your father's office and fighting with you, okay?"

"Sure."

"Thank you. Can I ask you something?"

"Is this going to hurt?" He tried to inject humor into his voice. He used to be able to make her laugh even at the worst times.

Her smile spread wide and full for the first time. "Probably."

"Let me have it, then."

"Are you sad to see your father sell this house?"

He looked around. "Honestly? Not at all. It hasn't been home in a long time. What pisses me off is my father wanted to throw out all my mother's things he had shoved into the attic and had no plans to tell me. If I hadn't come home, I wouldn't even have known the house was for sale."

"Why did you come home? Are you taking a vacation or something?"

"It doesn't matter why I'm home. I'm glad I'm here so I can save my mom's things. She kept journals and scrapbooks. Her handwriting is all over that stuff. I want it, and my father thinks it's garbage."

"I think your mom would like that. She was always so sentimental. Do you remember the blanket she knitted for the baby?"

Mom had knitted a beautiful white baby blanket with pink and blue shell-shaped edges. His mother had been so proud and excited to become a grandmother. His father had been anything but proud. He had actually asked him if Liv would consider terminating the pregnancy because they were so young.

"I do remember. That's long gone." He had searched for it after his mother had died, but could never find it. He would've liked to still have it.

"No, it isn't. I still have it."

"You do?"

She ducked her chin. "I do. It's one of my only possessions. I own next to nothing. I'm not like you. I could never plan long enough or well enough."

"Planning isn't all it's cracked up to be. All my planning didn't work out. Do you want to come upstairs? I've got a couple of folding chairs."

"I should go. It's getting dark, and I have to walk back to Mack's."

"I could drive you." He didn't want her to go just yet. They were finally getting somewhere.

"Thanks, but I think the fresh air will do me some good. It was nice to see you."

"Would you be interested in helping me go through the attic? It would go a lot faster with two of us. I have to be done by the end of the week."

"I don't know." She messed with the buttons on her camera, keeping her gaze away from his.

"Please. I could use the company, and my mom loved you. She wouldn't mind you going through her things." In another life, she would've been the person beside him, helping him with the changes. In another life, their now teenage son could help out too.

She went to the front door and opened it. He couldn't move as she went down the steps. She would walk away, and he would never see her. Hadn't he wanted to be with her again? Hadn't she been the one he wanted while he was in that hospital bed? He didn't know how to reach her.

She stopped and turned to him. "Could I take pictures while we worked?"

"Sure." He walked outside and stood before her because he needed to be close to her. For him, no time had passed. The ache in his heart when he looked at her was as strong in that moment as it had been all those years ago when she crossed his path for the first time. She had stolen his breath then and had again this morning.

"We could even dig up some of the history on the house. You could add it to a memory book along with whatever photos I take. It would be nice to have that information later in life."

It would be nicer if he had a child to hand it down to, but he couldn't say that. Maybe someday he would finally have a child, but he was through planning. If it happened, it happened.

"Wasn't the house built in the seventeen hundreds by some guy for his daughter to see the beach?" she said.

"You remember that?"

"I remember everything." Her words were barely a whisper.

Could he take this risk and allow her close to him? What would happen to his heart if she tore it in half again? He wasn't as strong as he had been. He was damaged goods now.

He closed the space between them and tilted her chin so she had to look up at him. The touch sent an electric current up his arm and through his chest. Her eyes pleaded with him.

For some reason she needed this as much as he did. But he needed something else. He needed her.

CHAPTER 6

*S*he had to stay sober. Hud could not know she had a problem. Well, she didn't have a problem really. She wasn't like other people who couldn't stop drinking. She could stop any time, but recently it had been harder to walk away. She needed to get ahead of her drinking before it took over.

She stood outside the old church built in the seventeen hundreds with its stone front worn down from centuries by the ocean and its tall gables that held nothing now but bats. The small property around the church was outlined with a wrought iron gate that creaked each time the wind played with it. The sun dipped in the sky, throwing gold and white stripes along the sidewalk.

A man huddled deep in his coat with a hat pulled

low on his head hurried past her and inside. She didn't really need to do this. She only had a few drinks at night. The nights were always long when she was alone. The nights had haunted her the most through the years. Her mind would take off and travel down roads she never wanted to visit when the world tucked itself behind closed doors in houses filled with families and love. Things she didn't have. That was why she had started drinking.

"Oh, fuck it," she muttered to herself and pushed her way in.

The meeting spot was in the basement of the church. A damp cold clung to the room with its linoleum floor and prison-gray walls. A circle of metal folding chairs, an arrangement found in a children's game of duck, duck, goose, waited for all those wanting to spill their ugliness like kitchen grease on the ground.

A few of the chairs were already taken. A man with ginger hair and gold chains around his neck fidgeted in his seat. He looked close to tears. A woman with eyes outlined in too much black eyeliner, a black leather jacket with spikes on the shoulder, and black boots up to her knees scowled at anyone who came near her. Another man, stocky build, with graying hair, and beady eyes took the seat next to the woman with the eyeliner. He was the man who passed her on the sidewalk. The eyeliner lady said something to him. He ignored her and sat down.

Liv hung back by the table with coffee and artificial creamer. She had never even been to a meeting like this before. There had never been a reason, until she had stood inches from Hudson, because she didn't have a problem. She wasn't like these people who tugged at their hair, whose eyes were sunken in their pallid-skinned faces.

Hudson always had his act together. He would disapprove of her choices since they split. She couldn't bear the idea of him thinking less of her. He already had plenty of reason to dislike her. But when he touched her face the other day, her entire body had sizzled. Only his touch could ever do that to her. No man had the magic to make her body sing the way he had. She had secretly cried many times after sex because she had missed him so much and it had been Hud she wanted in her bed. Not the guy she had been with. Except Darius. She had never cried with Darius.

"What are you doing here?" A male voice only inches from her ear startled her out of her thoughts. Hawk Egan towered over her with his large frame. Confusion floated over his chiseled face as he crossed his arms over his flannel-clad chest.

"Nothing. What are you doing here?" That was a stupid thing to say. Of course, she knew why he was there. She hadn't thought about Hawk showing up when she decided to come to a meeting. She should've found a place in another county instead of right in Water Course.

Hawk had sobered up. He wasn't ashamed of his illness. If he was going to attend a meeting, she should have realized it would be in his hometown where everyone loved and respected him, especially her oldest sister.

"What gives? Do you have a drinking problem?" he said.

"Why would you think that?"

"You're at a meeting for alcoholics. We're pretty friendly people, but this isn't exactly the social event of the month. Do you want to tell me what's really going on?" He poured coffee into a Styrofoam cup.

"I just...I..." She let out a long breath. She couldn't think of anything to say that would explain why she was there except the truth. She wasn't ready to admit to Hawk any of her failures. "Please don't tell Aria. No one knows I've been having some troubles lately. It's nothing I can't handle." Well, Phoenix and Mack suspected since she had shown up at their house in a dress covered in vodka, but she hadn't confirmed anything.

"Are you asking me to lie to my wife?" He stirred creamer into his coffee.

"Not lie exactly. Just don't mention you saw me here. I don't have a problem. I thought maybe I could use a little moral support is all." She only needed a little extra support. Her sisters were amazing and always there for her. She couldn't ask for a better family where they were concerned, but she had screwed up so many times around them. She didn't want to dive deeply into her recent indiscretions with them just yet.

"You have a bigger problem than you realize if you're asking me to keep secrets from Aria." He sipped his drink. The steam from the coffee swirled into the air around Hawk's face. She could turn that moment into a decent photograph, but she didn't have her camera. And she doubted Hawk would want her to take his picture.

She put a hand near her mouth to keep anyone from reading her lips. "I'm not like these people. I don't need to drink."

"You are exactly like these people. You have an illness. There is nothing to be ashamed of. With the right support, you'll be okay."

"I'm not ashamed. I just don't want anyone to know what I'm doing just yet. Please, Hawk. Don't say anything." She would tell her sisters if and when there was something to tell. For now, she wanted to check out the meeting because she could admit dumping a full punch bowl over her ex's head may have been a tad too much.

And there was the episode over the summer at

Mack and Phoenix's party. She had been a tad wasted when she showed up at Mack's house the other night too, but that had been because her landlord had delivered the eviction notice on the same night she found out Darius's girlfriend was pregnant.

His nostrils flared, and he shook his head. "Here's my deal. I'm on at the firehouse for the next forty-eight hours. I will give you a couple of days to come clean with Aria and Mack too. When I get home from my shift, I'm telling Aria whether you did or not. This is going to sound better coming from you."

"She'll be disappointed in me." Because her sisters expected her to always fall on her face. They seemed to think she couldn't take care of herself. And what if she never returned to a meeting? Why bother telling them about something that might not happen?

"She loves you and wants you happy and healthy. She'll understand." He took another sip and grimaced. "This tastes like shit. Two days, Liv. That's it." He found a seat next to the man with the ginger hair.

Hawk and his damn moral compass. He didn't understand what it was like for her. She only needed a little comfort to get through some rough spots. She could stop because she had never had a drinking problem before. She didn't even need this meeting. She would just not drink anymore.

Her situation was different than what he had been

through. He blamed himself for his brother Wyatt's death. She understood why Hawk had wanted to drink after that.

But he would tell Aria he had seen her, and she would tell Mack, and someone would call Blair and gossip. *Liv screwed up again. Liv will never get her act together. She doesn't even own a couch.* Staying in one place hadn't made sense to her because sitting still for too long helped the memories find her. She could dodge them if she moved around, kept her distance. At least that's what she thought until recently. Until she had bumped into Hud.

She stole a glance at the circle of chairs filling up. Maybe she and Hawk weren't that different after all. They both blamed themselves for the death of someone they loved. One chair remained open. She had nothing to talk about. Her problem was so far in the past it barely existed anymore. That awful night was just a memory.

She turned on her heel and went back out in the cold. The sun had set while she had been inside, and the wind had picked up off the ocean, mixing salt in the air. She dug her phone out of her jacket pocket and tapped at the screen with shaking fingers.

She held her breath until he answered.

"Hello?"

"Hud, it's me. I was wondering if you wanted to

grab something to eat. I mean if you haven't had dinner yet. It might be too late. Or we could grab a drink and talk about your plans for the stuff in your attic." Her words tangled in a spider's web of anxiety.

She had lost her mind when she agreed to work with him the other day at his house. Being near him had short circuited her brain. He had smelled so good, like fresh air and all male. But she didn't want to back out. Spending time with him was selfish, but she needed to be near him if only for a little while.

He choked out a laugh. "Hi to you too. I just made some pasta. It's not much, but I have plenty to share if you want to come by. I arranged the boxes in piles and numbered them all. I made a spreadsheet to document whatever's inside each one. I could show you."

Her smile bumped into the phone. Of course, Hud made a spreadsheet. "That sounds great. I'll grab a bottle of wine." She couldn't go empty-handed, and she wouldn't even have one glass.

"I don't really drink anymore except for the occasional beer. Just bring yourself."

"Really? Are you on a diet or something?" Hud had always enjoyed a good bottle of wine. He used to read wine magazines so he could have as much knowledge about the varieties as possible.

"Or something. I'll see you soon. And, Liv, I'm glad you called." He ended the conversation.

She stared at her phone for a second. Dinner with

Hud. She needed that more than she needed some meeting inside a cold basement with people she didn't know. She glanced at the stone church. Hawk was wrong. She was different, and since she hadn't stayed for the meeting, there wasn't anything to tell her sisters. He was off the hook. And so was she.

CHAPTER 7

The waves crashing against the beach became her lulling soundtrack as she made her way to Hud's. The rhythmic water soothed her soul. The ocean and the sand were in her blood, but she had stayed away, afraid she'd get pulled into the undertow of bad memories.

Walking in the cold cleared her head. She preferred to walk even in January because of all her years in the city where she hadn't needed a car and in her little town of Water Course where everything seemed just a block away.

Hud's old Victorian stretched into the black sky. She couldn't believe the house would belong to someone else soon. She had expected to be relieved that a new family would make better memories there, but she wasn't relieved at all.

Somehow knowing the house was always here waiting for her to show up gave her a sense of comfort. This was the last place she was with her son, and the only place he was when he wasn't inside her. She believed she would be able to come here when she was ready, but that could not happen now. New owners would never understand her desire to sit in a room where her son had died.

She rang the bell on the back door to save Hud the trip through the office. Friends and family came around back, and she had been that once, even if she wasn't that now. When Mrs. Lozado had opened the door to her with love in her eyes and a bright smile on her face, Liv would sometimes want to cry because no one had ever looked at her like that. Except maybe Hud, but his looks were filled with young love and lust. She was pretty sure she had devoured him with the same kind of facial expressions.

"Hi. Come on in." Hud held the door open wide, startling her for a second because her thoughts had run away and crashed into hot, steamy sex memories of him. "I was wondering if you were still going to show up." His smile broke wide across his face and danced in his dark eyes.

His black t-shirt stretched across his chest and biceps. His faded jeans hugged his legs in all the right places. His feet were bare.

"I stopped to get these." She handed over a bakery

box tied with a red and white string. "Like I said, I couldn't come empty-handed." She had made a quick stop at Mack's house first complaining of having a sweet craving.

Mack brought home cookies and cakes from the bakery that hadn't sold that day. She couldn't resell anything. She often gave food to her employees to take home, or she would donate it to the food bank. When she had enough, Mack brought the extras home to the boys and Phoenix. Liv grabbed some cookies to bring to Hud and a few sticky hugs from her nephews before heading over. Cookies were a better choice than wine.

"These are Mack's. I hope it's her oversized chocolate chip." He tapped the logo on the top of the box. "Thanks. Come on up." He led the way back into his family's kitchen.

The place smelled of lemon and polish. The floor had been swept and mopped. A small card table and two chairs sat in the spot where the round oak table used to be. In the center was a small mason jar with sprigs of parsley.

"Do you always make garnishes a focal point of the table?" She smiled, hoping he would know she liked it and wasn't being her snarky self. The centerpiece gesture was sweet, something Hud would do. She had grown used to his thoughtful ways like when he would go into the convenience store for milk and come out with a rose for her.

"The table needed something since I was having a guest. It was all I had on short notice." He shrugged and busied himself with grabbing paper plates from the small pile on the corner of the counter.

"It was very thoughtful. Thank you." She wanted to believe he actually was trying to impress her, and it wasn't simply Hud being Hud.

"Have a seat. Sorry about the paper and plastic. I wasn't expecting the house to be empty when I got here."

"I don't mind." She had eaten straight from the pot on nights she was by herself. What was the point in dirtying more dishes just for herself?

"Seriously, Liv, sit. I'll serve."

"You don't have to do that." She stood by the chair, unsure of what to do. She could help him so it didn't seem as if she had expected him to bring over her food. As much as she appreciated the parsley, wanted to be the reason he put it there, this night wasn't a date, and she didn't want him acting as if it were because the idea of a date made her stomach twist around the frazzled nerves she had before she arrived.

"I want to. It isn't often I have a beautiful woman at my table for dinner." He gave her that impish smile of his. Her heart picked up speed. The room was suddenly too warm.

"Why are you being so nice to me?" The biting

words slipped out. She should learn to tie her mouth shut or at least think before she spoke.

He stared at her with wide eyes. "You called me, remember? And you agreed to rummage around in my attic like we were old friends. I didn't force you here or into my life. Now that you are planted firmly in my presence, are you going to do that thing you do?"

"What thing is that?" She really didn't know what he was talking about. She had spent her life listening to her father tell her about the laundry list of things she had done wrong. She wasn't smart like Aria, or talented like Mack, or as nice as Blair. Hud would have plenty to pick from.

"That shove-me-away thing. I just want to be friends while I'm in town, Liv. I'm not asking you for anything. Why is that so hard for you?"

"I don't know." Because her feelings for him scared her even after all these years. Because she often wondered what he even saw in her when he could've had anyone he wanted. Because if she loved him, he would leave her like every other person she had loved in her life including their child. Lasting love didn't seem to be in the cards for her.

"You and I were on the same side back then. You weren't the only one hurting. We could've helped each other through a difficult time, but you pushed me away." He dropped the plates on the table with enough force to make some food spilled off the sides.

She wasn't hungry anymore. She wanted to go, to flee from this house, run home and put her head under a pillow. She didn't want to have this conversation now. "I made a mistake coming here."

"There she goes, sprinting for the door."

She hesitated with her hand on the knob. She had been the one to call him because he made her feel safe and that scared her. If she needed him too much, she feared he would pull out the safety net at the last second and destroy her. Handing over her vulnerability was a death sentence.

"Don't run out on me. I've been waiting a long time to say some of this to you." His voice was a whisper. She turned because his pain sent shivers over her skin. He scratched at his beard. The new look was unconventional for him, and it made her want to reach out and run her fingers over his jaw.

"I won't run anymore."

"Why is the sight of me so unbearable?"

His words punctured her gut. He was so wrong. "I never said that to you."

"You didn't have to." He dropped into the chair and stabbed the pasta with his fork.

"How can you be here, with me, and not be bothered by what happened?" She had wanted to grieve with him back then, but being near him had made it impossible. He had wanted to forge on, and all she had wanted was to fall apart.

"Do you mean how do I live my life without our son?" He arched his brow.

Those two little words, *our son*, wormed their way under her skin and tore her heart in two. He hurt as much as she did, but she hadn't been able to deal with his pain because he didn't break down. She had wanted him to come apart at the seams the same way she had so she wouldn't feel like such a failure.

"We were supposed to be parents. The whole world tipped on its end that day, and it won't right itself. How can you sit there eating pasta like it's no big deal?" She shouldn't want to fight with him, but she did. He had bottled up his emotions the minute they buried him. She wanted Hud to react in some way she could relate to.

He tossed the fork on the table. It hit the plate and fell to the floor. "Is that what you think? You think it isn't a big deal for me? There hasn't been a day that has gone by that I don't think about him, about us. If I had only gotten home sooner, maybe it would've been me who took you to the hospital. If I hadn't returned to school that semester, I could've taken care of you. God, Liv, why do you always think you're the only one who suffers? You don't have the market on loss."

Pain etched lines around his mouth and filled his eyes with tears. Her breath caught at the sight of them. He ran his hand through his hair, tugging at the ends.

She had done that to him. She had caused him anguish. She wanted him to fall apart, well here it was.

"I'm sorry I lost our baby. It wasn't your fault. Even if you had been beside me, I still would have failed."

He pushed out of the chair and came to her. He cupped his warm hands on her face. "It wasn't your fault either."

"But I was the mother. I was supposed to take care of him. I let him down. I let you down." Tears filled her eyes. She willed them away, but they betrayed her and burned hot streaks down her face.

He wiped a tear away with his thumb. "You didn't let anyone down, Livvie. It was an accident. Stop blaming yourself."

His warmth and his strength seeped from him and wrapped around her like a thick blanket. She wanted to cocoon herself in him and never let go. "Hud..." Her voice snagged on her tears. She swallowed and tried again. "I want to stop hurting all the time." She wanted to unload everything that had happened to her lately. She was tired of carrying the burden alone. She was a screwup. She always had been.

"How can I help you?"

"Why do you want to do that?" She hadn't expected him to offer her any kind of help. She wasn't sure she was even ready to let her heart go willingly to him. He represented the past and the pain it caused. She would be smart to move on, forget about Hud. She should start over somewhere else, without him and the constant reminders. Except she had never been able to do that. She needed to start being honest about something, and her feelings for him were it.

"I want to help you, because I still love you."

She stared at him, unsure if she had heard him correctly. After all this time? She had to be sure before she made a fool of herself and said it too. But she wanted to say it even while she was having thoughts of running away because no matter what had happened, she had always loved him. "What did you say?"

He backed away. "I shouldn't have said that. I'm sorry. I don't know what came over me. You were upset. You don't want to hear that. Forget I said it."

"Wait a second. I don't want to forget it—"

"I know you don't love me. At least not since that night. No matter what you said right now, you still think I should've done something to save him. You don't have to throw it in my face."

"Will you shut up for a minute? I don't want to forget what you said because I love you too." Her words echoed in the space. Her heart still raced, and an awful heat ran over her body. But she hadn't come apart. In fact, her shoulders dropped for the first time in weeks.

He stared at her with his mouth half open and not saying anything. She held her breath and begged her feet to stay put. Her phone went off and shattered the silence.

She should ignore it and let Hud respond to her declaration, but she was supposed to be on call for any accidents. She couldn't afford to lose this job. "I'm sorry. I have to get that. It could be Milly."

"Sure." He turned away and dumped the food in the garbage.

The phone screen confirmed what she thought. "Hey, Milly."

"There's a car crash down on Beach Avenue. Go take some photos. I want to see the accident site, not just the vehicles. And send them to me tonight. Don't forget, Liv. This is important."

"I got it. Stop your haranguing." She ended the call. "I have to go. It was work."

"Okay. I'll see you." He stayed on the other side of the kitchen, leaning against the counter.

"That's it? You're not going to say anything about what I just said?" She had blurted out the most intimate thing she could have.

"You're leaving. I don't think now is the time." He was going to allow her to drown in embarrassment.

"I could come by tomorrow to help you with the attic." Her words held a note of desperation even to her. She didn't want this night to end. She wanted to rewind to right before Milly ruined everything. After all these years, Hudson Lozado still loved her. Luck had finally turned in her direction, but she didn't deserve it. Not after how she treated him.

"You could come back after you're done." He gave her that impish grin again.

"You want me to?"

"You just told me you loved me. I think we have more to talk about."

"I don't know how long I'll be."

"I'll wait up."

CHAPTER 8

*B*each Avenue was a line of blue and red lights swirling in ribbons against the night sky. Firetrucks and police cars were parked in front of the boardwalk. Even two tow trucks were present. The ocean kept its rhythm despite the cars mangled together. Nothing stopped the power of the ocean, which was only made more beautiful by the moon's white rays on its surface. Liv snapped a quick picture of the sky and ocean before making her way through the crowd.

Both her brothers-in-law stood by the firetruck. Phoenix in his fire gear and Hawk the way she had left him at the meeting. She wanted to avoid them but wouldn't be able to. Better to get the pleasantries out of the way.

"Hey, guys."

"Oh, good, you're here to take photos," Phoenix said. "Milly sent a text, saying you were on the way."

"Of course, she did, the micro-manager. Did anyone get hurt?" Because she didn't want to take any pictures of someone still in the car bleeding and stuck under the dashboard. There wasn't enough money on the planet for that.

"Everyone is out of the cars. The driver of the sedan is over there. And the woman with the mini-van is sitting on the bench." Hawk pointed at each one.

"Thanks." She eased away to get a better look at the wreckage. She took pictures from different angles, making sure Milly got what she needed. She even included the broken glass on the street, and the tow truck driver who waved when she pointed her camera in his direction.

The man who owned the sedan faced the ocean, his arms crossed over his chest. His hair was long and wavy and his beard thick. His body was well-toned, but not bulky. He wore flip-flops even though the night was cold. A single tear ran down his face.

She lifted her camera to view him through the finder. His mouth turned down. He shivered against the wind. His head shook ever so slightly. She would've missed it if she hadn't had her camera. He was deep in thought and unaware of her. The way she liked her subjects. When they let their guards down, they could be themselves. She used to be good at making that happen for them. She used to be very good at what she did, but she had grown bored and frustrated by her industry. Art had taken a backseat to dollars. She had never become a photographer because of the money. She had wanted to tell stories with her camera, and behind the camera she wasn't the weird girl whose father abused her. She could say things with her camera she couldn't with her mouth. People often liked her photos better than the things that she said.

She snapped away, hoping to capture his pain under the light of the moon. He turned with the beat of the flash.

"Are you taking my picture?" He swiped at his face.

"Um. I am. I'm sorry. You are so fascinating to watch. Hasn't anyone ever told you that?"

"No. Why would they? Isn't taking pictures without someone's permission against the law or something? Are you with some tabloid rag?" He searched over his shoulder for some kind of answer.

"I'm Liv Scirocco. I work for *Fluent Magazine*. I don't have a card on me at the moment." She had worked at *Fluent* until her boss fired her for holding a crying baby in a nursery. She doubted this guy would call human resources and check. The current issue still had her work in it. He would see the photo credits if he wanted to bother.

She threw out the magazine's name to sound legitimate. She couldn't very well tell the man she worked for the other woman's insurance company. Milly had sent a text with the details of the mini-van; otherwise, she would have no idea who the client was.

"Are you going to sell those pictures?" He raked a hand through his hair.

"No. I just couldn't help myself. I had to capture you. You're...well, this might sound silly, but you're beautiful. And the expression on your face in the moonlight tells a thousand stories."

"You saw all that from me standing here freezing my ass off, crying like a baby?" He coughed out a laugh.

"It's what I do," she said with a shrug. It may not make sense to him or most people, but what she saw in him tonight was the reason she was driven to take pictures.

She had started taking photos in high school for the yearbook. The activity gave her something to do after school that didn't cost money and kept her out of the house. When the popular kids saw her coming with her camera, they would beg to have their pictures taken. No one bullied her when she had her camera. But she had always preferred to take photos of the kids who were unsuspecting, the ones who wanted to blend in. They were far more interesting.

"You're crazy, lady."

"I can send them to you if you want."

"No, thanks. I want as few reminders of this night as possible."

Someone called his name because he turned and ran into the arms of a woman with a blue scarf tied around her head. At least this woman had had the sense to wear shoes with a toe.

Liv stood there a little longer until this mystery person and his companion huddled into her bright-green car and drove away.

The mangled cars had been towed. The police had left the scene. The last of the firefighters climbed onto the truck. She waved to Hawk and Phoenix. She wanted to get to her computer and see the images. An electric current ran over her skin. That feeling hadn't happened at work in ages. The last time she had been excited about her job had been eons ago.

She sent Hud a text.

I have some work to do. Come by Mack's house in an hour.

Her phone pinged.

Have a headache. Can I take you to breakfast tomorrow?

He didn't want to see her. He was probably just being nice. She shouldn't be surprised. Too many years and too many bad memories were between them. They couldn't pick back up where they left off as if nothing had happened. Throwing words like love around without any consideration was dangerous. She hadn't thought before she spoke them. His hands on her face, the tender way he had brushed her tear away made her forget he wasn't hers. She hadn't trusted him to be there for her after their son died. Instead of just saying that, she broke his heart until it was unrepairable.

Feel better. I'll call you.

Which she wouldn't.

HUD DRAGGED himself out of bed. He shouldn't have backed out on Liv, not after what they had said. Sure, the intimation of love had been in the heat of the moment, but he meant what he had said. Her skin under his touch had sent all the heat to his groin. He had an erection for the first time since the heart attack because of the way she had looked at him. He wanted to take the hurt away for her, but he was certain his rejection to visit her had led to her saying no to breakfast.

He pulled on a pair of sweatpants and a zip-up hoodie. It was late, but that couldn't matter. She wouldn't want to see him, but he had to see her. He did love her. Always. He hoped she had meant it too. At least in the moment.

He wasn't going to bother to call or text and give her the chance to turn him down again. He pulled the car out of the garage and headed over to Mack's house. Mack might hate him for waking her up in the middle of the night, probably try to throw him out on his ass, but hopefully she would understand what he was trying to do.

The house was dark except for one window in the front. Someone was up. He knocked on the door instead of the bell. If no one came to the door, he would go home and try again at a suitable hour.

He waited on the porch while the wind whipped in from the ocean. He would count to ten. If she didn't come out, then that was that.

"Eight, nine." The door opened and Liv stared at him with wide eyes. Her makeup had run making black half-moons on her skin. Her hair was piled on top of her head with some pieces hanging around her face. Her cheeks were flushed red.

"What are you doing here?" She leaned her head against the door and closed her eyes. It seemed as if those words cost her.

"Did I wake you?" He had allowed his heart to let him behave like a fool and come here ready to declare promises of a second chance.

"I thought you didn't feel well. Or was that code for not wanting to see me?" Her words slurred off her lips.

"Were you drinking?" He smelled the hint of alcohol drifting from her.

"I'm just tired. I've been working for hours. Go home, Hudson." She tried to close the door, but he didn't budge. He didn't buy her tired line.

"What are you working on?" He wouldn't give up

that easily. He had to at least try to tell her how he felt. But if she was too drunk to remember or just drunk enough to stay mad, he might be making a mistake.

"Just some photos. You didn't answer my question. Why did you blow me off?"

"Can I come in? It's cold out here. Or will I wake Mack and the boys?" He rubbed his arms to ward off the salt water spray in the wind. He probably should've worn a jacket.

"No one is here except me. Mack and the boys live with Phoenix now. Mr. Perfect. Have you met him?" She turned on her heel and went inside, swaying on her feet as if the floor rolled under her. Her fuzzy bathrobe floated in the air, revealing her bare legs. Her calves were toned and led into her tiny ankles. His groin moved again.

He followed her inside and closed the door. A half-empty bottle of vodka sat on the coffee table. Beside her open laptop was a full glass of the clear liquid and a bag of cheese doodles.

"What do you mean Mack and the boys live at Phoenix's now?"

She swiped a piece of white notebook paper from the table and held it out to him. "My sister and her perfect fiancé packed up with the boys and moved into Phoenix's place to give me space. She left me this note so I wouldn't be frightened when I returned. He's selling his house too, by the way, so they can live here

84

as one big happy family." She waved her hand in the air. The paper slipped from her fingers and floated to the ground. Liv stared at it as if she were seeing it for the first time. She swayed more.

"That's a very nice gesture."

"It's just like Mack to always do something so nice. She gave me her car to use too. How will I ever repay her?" She flopped onto the couch. Her legs flew up and gave him a pretty good view of her black panties. He stifled a groan.

"How much have you had to drink?"

"Do you think I might be drunk? Is it the vodka? My perfect soon-to-be brother-in-law, Phoenix, the bossy one, thinks I drink too much. Did he mention that to you? He told me so just the other morning." She held up the bottle. "Do you want some? I don't mind sharing."

"I've known the Egans for many years, but we haven't spoken recently. Phoenix would be the first one to tell you he isn't perfect." Observant maybe, but definitely not perfect.

"Oh, he is. He'll do anything for Mack, including risk his life to save hers. He did that, you know. This very house caught fire last year. He found a way to save her. It's so perfect it's nauseating."

She poured more vodka into her already full glass. Some spilled over the side. She ran her tongue along the glass to stop the spillage. If this were another time that didn't involve a drunk Liv, he would find that move extremely sexy.

He sat beside her and eased the glass out of her hands. "You don't mean that. I know you like Phoenix."

"Yeah, how do you know that? Are you going to drink that?"

"No, and neither are you. And I know you like Phoenix because you have a big heart and you want Mack to be happy." He poured the vodka into the sink.

"Hey, that costs money." She waved a finger at him.

He stifled a smile. "I'll pay you back."

She laced her fingers in her lap. "I do want Mack to be happy. She deserves it after that asshat David. Mack and Aria lucked out in the man department. The next thing I know, Blair will call and say she found true love too. Speaking of which, I haven't heard from my sister in days. I think Blair is blowing me off." She grabbed her phone and swiped at the screen.

He eased the phone out of her hand, much like the glass, before she called Blair and woke her for no good reason. "She's probably sleeping."

"Whatever. You know, I'm the only one who can't get her act together. No man will want me knowing what I did to you. I'm not worth getting involved with because I hurt everyone I love."

She had put her guard up after their son died, and as hard as he had tried, he couldn't break through it. He had driven to the city countless times trying to get her to speak to him. He had stood outside her apartment building shouting to the windows until the police came. He tried to tell her what he would do to make their life right, but she had said she didn't want to be with him anymore. She didn't love him anymore. "You don't hurt everyone you love."

"That coming from you. Give me a break, Hudson. I hurt you because I lost your baby, and I broke up with you on top of that. Why are you here? Please go." She reached for the bottle.

"Do you feel like having some coffee with me?" He held it away from her. There wasn't any point in arguing with her at the moment because she wouldn't listen to reason. She hadn't hurt him because they lost the baby. She hurt him because she refused to grieve with him.

She had broken his heart when she had left him, but he didn't blame her for what had happened. His father had explained the complications with the delivery. The weather had been terrible. They couldn't get to a hospital so his father had brought Liv to his office instead. They needed medical equipment and a staff he hadn't had in his small-town office.

"I'm not drunk, Hud." She reached for the bottle.

"Yeah, you are."

"Are you going to lecture me too? Because you can save it. Give me the bottle." She leaned across him to grab the bottle. Her breasts pressed against his chest, and wisps of her hair tickled his face. Every nerve went on high alert, but he would never act on it. Not tonight with the way she was.

"No." He put the bottle on top of the fridge. "Let's go get some coffee. I wanted to talk to you."

"What is there to talk about?" She pulled her robe closed.

"We said some things earlier." He sat beside her again.

"The I love you stuff. I know you didn't mean it. Don't worry about it." She waved him away.

He let out a long breath. "I needed to see you. I wanted you to know I wasn't making up the headache. I'm wasn't trying to dodge our conversation. I haven't been feeling well, recently."

"You're dying, aren't you? I knew it from earlier when you went all white and almost passed out."

He quelled a laugh. The crease between her brows indicated she was serious; if he laughed at her worry, she would get mad at him. "No, sweetheart, I'm not dying. At least not today."

"I'm glad." She leaned back into the corner of the couch and pulled the blanket over her. The crease between her brows smoothed out.

He tucked the blanket around her bare legs. Her skin was cool to his touch. Touching her led him into dangerous territory. He forced any more thoughts about her skin away.

"How about if I start a fire? Then we can talk until you fall asleep." The wind made its way down the chimney and chilled the small living space.

He would tell her why he had the headache, but not tonight. Tonight, he would sit with her for a while, take care of her if she needed something. He would prefer to sleep in the chair just to be near her, but she would probably tell him to go home.

"There's nothing to talk about. I don't need a fire. I have the blanket." She snuggled further into the cushions.

She hadn't exactly given him the command to leave. Instead, he gathered the firewood and the pieces of kindling by the hearth. Warming up the room was the least he could do for her. The fire started to take life, and he sat back on the couch. Her eyes were still closed.

"Liv, are you asleep?"

"Go home, Hud. You're wasting your time with me." Her eyes remained closed.

"How about if I stay until you fall asleep? We can talk tomorrow." Okay, there was the direct order, but she shouldn't be left alone. He had no idea how much she had had to drink. Anything could happen.

"I don't want you here." She finally looked at him.

"Why not?" He would make her say her reasons, and he would do his best to find solutions to her objections.

"Because you will see me for who I truly am and fall

out of love with me. You weren't supposed to find me like this."

He laced his fingers through hers. "I know who you are, and I will always love you." He would shout it from every roof in Water Course if that's what it took to make her believe him. He would paddle out to the horizon on that stupid surfboard he bought if he could convince her she had always been the one. He had gone on with his life because she had forced him to, but every woman he was with failed his comparison test. She was in his blood and his soul. He couldn't shake free of her any more than the sun could stop rising.

"Please stop saying you love me." She pulled her hand away. "I don't want to disappoint you again."

"You could not possibly. Damn it, Liv, even if I never say I love you again, I still mean it. And you said it to me not four hours ago. Did you lie to me?" He held his breath.

She closed her eyes again. "I've never lied to you."

"Then you still love me." He gave himself permission to hope.

"So what? My life is a mess. I don't have a decent job or a place to live. And according to you and everyone else, I drink too much. Why would you want that when you have your shit together?" Each word lost more steam than the one before like a train pulling into the station.

He opened his mouth to tell her about the heart

attack and quitting his job, but he stopped. Tonight wasn't the time for a conversation like that. She needed to sleep it off, and maybe another time they could talk more.

"I don't have anything together. Believe me. Why don't you get some sleep? I'll stay until you do."

"Suit yourself." She turned on her side, away from him, and tugged the blanket up to her ears. He would take that as a win because if she really wanted him to leave, she would've dragged him to the door. Drunk or not.

He would stay until her breathing evened out and he could be certain she was asleep and all right. Being with her, even if she was a little drunk, eased the ache in his chest. Watching her sleep was as natural as breathing.

He glanced at her laptop opened to a photo app. Pictures were displayed in galley style on the screen.

"Can I look at your photos?" Browsing some of her photos would help him pass the time and maybe even get a small insight into what she had been up to recently. Whatever it was, it hadn't healed her demons. "Liv?"

She didn't answer him.

"Sweetheart, are you sleeping?"

Her breathing had slowed. She had finally fallen

asleep. She would need the rest after tonight. He pulled the laptop closer. He would only look at the photos on the screen. He wouldn't click on anything.

The shots were of a car accident. He assumed the one she went to after she had left his place. The mangled metal looked menacing. He hoped no one was hurt. The photo of the man staring at the ocean stopped his hand over the track pad. The guy's face was stoic. He could be thinking anything in that moment. But it was the single tear against the man's leathered skin that Liv had captured, almost like the focal point, that showed the pain he was in. He didn't know the first thing about photography other than to point his phone at something and hit the button. But he knew without a doubt that Liv had been gifted with a camera.

She was something special. She used to snap photos of him when he wasn't looking, usually studying, and make him appear as if he had the world on his shoulders. During those times, he had. She had said she loved that side of him, his philosophical side she called it. But she wouldn't let him stay that way for too long. She would come over to him push him away from the table and straddle him. Her lips could make him forget his studies and his worries. She either had to make him laugh or take him to bed in those moments. He was happy either way.

He had let her down after their son died. He

should've stuck harder, making her see they could've still built a life together. They could've tried again. He should've done for her what she had done for him so many times. He hadn't taken her pain away. He had caused her more, and that was the reason she had left him. She deserved better than him.

He closed the laptop and tucked the blanket around her again. Her breathing was deep. The lines between her brow had smoothed out. His Livvie was getting some much-needed peace.

He placed a light kiss on her head. "No more I love yous."

And let himself out into the cold.

CHAPTER 9

*L*iv blinked against the sunlight streaming through the window. Her body ached from head to toe. Falling asleep on the couch had been a mistake, but her head had been spinning, and Hud was there keeping her safe.

She sat up. No sign of Hud existed except for the ashes in the fireplace and the vodka bottle on the top of the refrigerator. He must've waited until she fell asleep and left. She rubbed the heels of her hands into her eyes. She hadn't meant to drink so much. She had only two glasses, but she hadn't eaten any dinner. The booze went straight to her head.

After she had emailed the accident photos to Milly, she studied the photo of that guy staring at the ocean. What had he lost that night in the accident? Or had something else driven him to that much distress?

94

Every time she looked at him staring off into space with that single tear running down his face, chills ran over her spine. She hadn't been able to really figure out why this photo was so different, but then she went back and looked at her other work. She had been uninspired for a long time. She hadn't captured much of the people she had photographed other than the clothes they wore and the makeup on their faces. There had been no heart and soul in her work because she didn't have either to work with.

She pushed off the couch and eyed the vodka. "Don't do it." And went into the bathroom and turned the shower to cold.

She wanted to take more pictures like last night. She wanted to create art that was true and honest again. She also wanted to find Hud this morning and have that talk. She wished he had stayed the night, but that might be wishing for too much. She was pretty sure she had tried to throw him out. She couldn't really expect him to stick around for more of that.

She showered and dressed quickly. Hud might even be still asleep if she hurried over to his place. Or maybe he had gone surfing. She'd wait until he came back. They could work in the attic today side by side. With their hands busy, it would be easier to talk about those uncomfortable things they had avoided. Well, she had avoided them.

Her phone rang as she locked the front door. The

cold morning and the ocean wind collided with her on the porch and knocked her off-balance. Her hair blew across her face, blocking her view as she dug for her phone in her purse.

Milly's name lit up the screen. She should ignore the call. Say she was in the shower or something in a text to her later, but she didn't want to prove Phoenix right in his opinion of her.

"Hey, Milly. Did you get my photos?" She hurried down the steps. She would take the car and save time even though a brisk walk would clear the fog in her brain still lingering even after the cold shower.

"I did. Thanks. I'm calling because there was a four-alarm fire out on Jackson Street. An insurance inspector won't be called in for a few days, but I want to see photos of the outside now. Go on over and take what you can without getting in the way. Those firemen worked hard to put that fire out. I don't want you causing them any trouble."

"Why would I do that?"

"I'm no dummy. I know you lost your last job because you broke into a nursery. I took a chance on you because of Phoenix. He's the one I trust with my life." Milly ended the call.

"I didn't break in, you dumb bird," she said to no one.

She tossed the phone onto the front seat of the car and headed to Jackson Street. Hud would have to wait.

But for the first time in a long time, she was excited about going to work.

THE SMELL of burnt wood and smoke filled the air. The top half of an old Victorian house was covered in soot. The front windows were blown out. Glass, clapboard, and ashes littered the front lawn like wounded confetti.

Spectators stood on the sidewalk hunkered down in their coats, pointing and talking. Some held up their phones, taking pictures or videos that would show up on social media in seconds. Everyone would want to know what started the fire. Liv just wanted some photos.

The firetruck idled at the curb. Two firefighters dressed in their gear folded up the hose. Hawk barked out some orders to the men who nodded in response. He had been promoted about a year ago to the in-charge guy. He really had pulled his life together. Maybe those meetings were helpful.

"Hey, Hawk." She would say hello and then get to work, but she would not bring up the day before when she ditched the meeting.

"Liv. What are you doing here?" His face was covered in streaks of soot. His hair stuck up in odd places.

"Milly sent me. Is it okay if I grab a few photos from the yard? I won't touch anything or go near the house."

"I will never understand why Milly has to have photos of the fire the day it happens. She can still see all the damage after we clear out of here." He tucked his helmet under his arm.

"Do you know what started the fire?"

"Looks electrical. Old wiring in these houses can go up quickly. It's a shame. This one was supposed to be on the walking tour in a few months. It won't be on it now. You can take your pictures. If anyone complains, tell them I said it was okay."

"Thanks. Is the owner here?"

Hawk pointed to an older man and a woman huddled together. She wore a pink flannel nightgown and snow boots on her feet as if she hadn't had a chance to dress for the day before the fire took off. The woman clutched a picture frame to her chest. The husband, assuming it was her husband, wrapped an arm around her hunched shoulders. He only had on a white undershirt with his pot belly hanging over his jeans. His skinny arms were covered with wrinkled skin. He shivered in the cold.

"I have to finish up here. I'll see you later, and remember, you need to tell Aria what's going on with you." He didn't wait for her to respond, but sauntered back to the men with the hose. He and Phoenix had the same walk, confident with a hint of arrogance. She liked Hud's stride better.

She didn't have anything to tell Aria. Sometimes she had too much to drink, but it was only when she was alone and late at night. Last night, when Hud had found her a little wasted, she had been hurt when she found out that Mack and the boys were gone. She didn't want to be alone right now. Mack was just trying to be nice by giving her space to roam around and a bed to sleep in, but she would have preferred the house filled with noise and Ian and Elliott waking her up each morning. All she wanted was to matter, to be a part of something special.

She shook the pitying thoughts away. She could visit them at Phoenix's house, and maybe it would sell quickly and they'd come back. Of course, there was also Hud. Hud had always made her feel special. She should have appreciated that more.

Liv picked her way across the debris on the lawn for some close-ups of the house. She concentrated on the windows and doors. The backyard was untouched by the flames. From the back, no one would even know there had been a fire. She suspected the inside would tell a different story, and Milly would want that one documented too, but not today. She didn't want to inconvenience the firefighters. Milly's words shouldn't bother her, but their sharp bite hurt just the same. So, she had lost her job. She would pick that crying baby up all over again. If the nurses had been there, she would've minded her own business, but a newborn shouldn't be afraid.

Returning to the front yard, she moved to the other side of the street to capture the top of the house with its broken siding and burned-out roof. The woman in the pink nightgown still holding the picture frame stepped onto the lawn and weaved her way through the debris.

Liv focused her camera on the woman and snapped pictures. She kept her distance, inching toward the corner of the property beside an old oak tree. She didn't want to be noticed. She wanted the woman to express herself in whatever way she needed to.

She zoomed the camera's focus onto the woman's face and captured the lines of well-lived years, and the whites of her knuckles as she continued to grip that frame. Her curiosity was piqued. What was that picture? Maybe of her wedding day or a shot of her children posed in front of the fireplace. Whatever it was, the devastation of this fire had made itself clear as the woman sat down on the soaked lawn amongst the rubble that was once her life and soul and sobbed.

Liv wiped a tear from her eye. She wasn't the only one with so much pain it hurt to breathe. Suffering was everywhere, and it deserved to be noticed and cared for. She wanted to be the one to do it, but she wasn't sure if she was still good enough.

The firetruck pulled away and dragged her attention after it. The engine's roar diminished as it rolled down the street and the stillness replaced it. Hawk had been hurting once, but he was good now. His men respected him. Her sister loved him. He was a good dad, something he had known nothing about before becoming a father. Those meetings had helped him clean up his act and get Aria back. She could try too, if only for her work. Because she wasn't sure if she had much else.

CHAPTER 10

*H*ud climbed the stairs to the attic of his home with a large cup of coffee in his hand. He was supposed to cut out caffeine, but after the night he had of tossing and turning, and the rough session of falling off his surfboard, he figured his heart wouldn't mind too much.

After he left Liv's place, he had come home, but he couldn't sleep. Thoughts of her had crashed around in his head like the ocean during a storm. She had said she loved him and had never meant to push him away, but what did that really mean? She had been half asleep and drunk when she said the second part.

He had hoped an hour on his board would clear his head a little, but he couldn't stay focused and had lost his patience with waiting for a good wave. When he finally caught one, he fell off and embarrassed himself.

Some of the other surfers had had a good laugh at his expense.

The wind howled outside and rattled the small attic windows. He pulled up the zipper of his hoodie and sipped his coffee. Boxes of all shapes and sizes filled the attic in every dark corner. His father had kept old furniture with broken legs and backs. Black garbage bags filled with who knew what sat atop old luggage that hadn't seen the inside of an airport in probably forty years.

Even though he had made a spreadsheet with the box numbers, he didn't know where to begin. Much like he didn't know how to read Liv. Maybe it would be better if they didn't explore those unresolved feelings. Two people who had been victims of the same tragedy couldn't possibly work, could they? The tragedy would always exist between them, or would it?

He needed a distraction from thoughts of Liv and dug his phone out of his pocket. He scrolled through his contacts until he found his father. The phone rang and rang. He expected the call to switch over to voicemail.

"Hello?"

"Hey, Dad. Why didn't you sell the house right after Mom died?" He put the phone on speaker and started cutting open a box.

He had always wondered why his father remained

living here. He could've rented out the apartment, but he had never loved this house the way his mother had.

His mother had been the one to keep things neat and clean. She ironed bed sheets and swept the floors daily. She hummed while she dusted and polished the appliances. His father had wanted the picture-perfect image of his family and home for others to see, but he didn't want to do the work it involved.

"What kind of a question is that?" His father's voice was rushed and tight as if he was trying to control himself, but failing at hiding his unhappiness.

"The kind that deserves an answer." He lifted out an old train set he had as a kid. The box was filled with his toys. All of this could go in the garbage. He didn't want any of his old toys.

Appearances had been important to his father. He wanted everyone in town to believe they were the perfect family. No one could know his mother slept in the guestroom most of his life or how his parents fought about everything. Outside of the house they smiled and laughed at each other's jokes. They would share looks or touches that presented a happy marriage, but behind closed doors they slammed dishes and doors.

She had thought he wasn't aware of their fights, but he was. His father would come upstairs after a long day of seeing patients and start drinking wine. His parents would fight. He would hide in his bedroom behind his bed with his hands over his ears. He had often wished for a sibling to share the burden of his parents' unhappiness with. It wasn't until he started to date Liv that he had someone he could trust enough to share what really went on behind closed doors.

Her home life was far worse than his had been and everyone in town knew about what went on in the Scirocco house. His parents and their unhappy marriage were a walk in the park compared to what she and her sisters went through.

"FINE. I had other things to worry about. You were in college. I needed to work to pay for your education."

His father had paid for school only if Hud majored in something practical. He had wanted to follow his passion for art and history, but his father said no. He picked finance instead but had hated every minute of it. It didn't matter how much money he had made, and he had made a ton. His wife took most of it in the divorce. He hadn't bothered to fight her. He had only wanted to be free. The heart attack gave him the final reason to toss his career away.

"Is there anything in the attic you actually want?" He moved the box of toys closer to the door.

"I told you I am throwing it all away. It's junk. I haven't been up there in years. If I needed something, I would've retrieved it or replaced it by now." His father hung up.

He stared at his phone for a minute. His father had always been an ungrateful, selfish bastard. But memories of his mother twisted the guilt in his stomach. She would've wanted him to make peace and help his father see this project through.

"Screw you, old man. I'm keeping everything up here whether you like it or not."

An angry car horn blew long and hard below the window. He looked out. Parked on the street was a small white pickup and a guy standing in the flatbed facing the house, waving his hands.

"I wasn't ready for this visit." He grabbed his coffee and hurried outside before Owen Hearst attracted too much attention.

"I rang the bell for ten minutes." Owen jumped down from his truck and crossed the yard in two strides. Owen leaned in for a hug, but he backed up.

"I was in the attic. I didn't hear it. What brings you by?" He had avoided contacting Owen since his return to town. Owen would want to get together, rehash old times, and catch up on the new. He had nothing worth contributing to a conversation like that. The last thing he wanted to do was remember the heart attack in full detail or admit to the crossroad he was standing at.

"The question, my man, is what are you doing in town? You didn't call or text. The last I heard from you was a month ago. Then I hear through the Water Course grapevine that *the* Hudson Lozado is staying in his old place and catching waves this morning. Not cool, man, that I have to hear it from the gossip chain and not my best friend." Owen pulled off his knit cap and scratched his head.

"I hadn't planned on staying more than a day or two." That wasn't a complete lie. He hadn't thought this stay would be long or worth noting. He assumed he would call Owen when he got to the next stop.

"Did you miss the salt air?" Owen dropped down on the porch steps and stretched out his legs.

"Something like that." He stayed in his place on the front walk. The sun tried to peek through the thick gray clouds. The few rays that fell on his face warmed him some and eased the chill in his bones from being in the attic.

"What exactly is it like?" Owen would probe for answers until he got some.

"I needed a change of pace. That's all."

"Are you saying you want to slow down?" Owen stood and searched his face.

He turned away. "I don't know. Maybe." He had no idea what he wanted to do anymore. A month ago, he was managing a life. It was a life he didn't exactly love, but it was working. He went to work, came home, worked out, and repeat. Once in a while he went out with friends. He could've done that for a while longer, but the heart attack happened and now nothing made sense.

Then he saw Liv and everything changed again. He could breathe for the first time in he couldn't remember when. She had the power to reset him, and he needed that.

"Come work with me." Owen twisted his hat.

"What do you need me for? You already have a bookkeeper." He hadn't been anything more than a glorified money manager working on Wall Street. If his clients had bothered to take the time, they could've done for themselves what he did for them. He was just good at guessing.

Owen shook his head. "Man, you are one stubborn ass who doesn't know his own worth. Because of you, I had the money to take my business to the next level. I can help way more people and beaches now."

"You would've been just fine without me. I should get back inside. I'm cleaning up the attic."

"I can't believe your dad is selling. I thought he'd work forever." Owen glanced up at the house.

"I thought so too."

"Do you want to catch some waves with me while you're here?"

"I'm sorry. I should've called you."

"Forget it. I'm flying out at the end of the month to help with a beach cleanup. Maybe you should take some time off and come along. It might help with those circles under your eyes." Owen pointed at his face.

"I didn't sleep well last night." He had been too preoccupied with thoughts of Liv.

"I can see that. Listen, man, I don't know what's going on with you right now, but I know when something's up. You have that ghost look on your face like you haven't seen the sun in a really long time. And you haven't returned my calls in the last two weeks."

"Sorry about that too." He hadn't called anyone since the heart attack except his dad who hadn't come up to the hospital to see him.

"Don't be sorry. Just say you'll come with me to clean up. I could use my friend out there with me, finally."

His lifetime friend had built a company that cleaned up the oceans and turned the plastic waste into jewelry. He had had a chance to get in on the ground floor, but it had been too risky, and he had still been reeling from losing Liv and the baby. For years it was all he could do to keep putting one foot in front of the other. It was no wonder he had married the wrong woman not long after.

"Wouldn't you rather just surf with me?" He shoved his hands in his pockets.

"I want to do both. Come on. What's there to think about? Sand. Surf. Philanthropy." Owen threw his hands in the air.

"Liv's in town." He kicked the ground. He was saying more than he had originally planned, but if he was going to be honest with himself, he missed Owen and his easy friendship. He needed someone in his corner these days.

"That explains it. The heart wants what the heart wants. Are you going for it this time?" Owen pulled his hat back on his head.

"I'm taking it slow." Because the last time he tried to convince her he loved her and wanted a life with her even without their child, she had made it clear she wasn't interested.

"Hudson, man, for once in your life, take a risk. What's the worst that could happen? Are you going to die if she tells you no?"

He almost died from the heart attack. Something he never saw coming. A genetic malfunction that was rare and caused his blood to clot too much. If his son had lived, he'd been a teenager now. They would have to test him for the gene. How would Liv feel about him giving their child a chance at a rare disease?

"Hopefully not today." He forced a smile he didn't feel.

"Don't wait. If you want that woman once and for all, go get her. Go get the life you were meant to have."

"What if she still doesn't want me?" She had practically thrown him out last night. He could blame her words on the booze, but weren't people usually more honest when they were drunk?

"She'd be a fool."

"Do you ever talk to Blair?" He didn't want to discuss Liv anymore. A long time ago, when life was less complicated, Owen and Blair had a hot and heavy thing.

Owen shook his head and walked back to the truck. "No way. That boat has sailed, never to be seen again. We were no good together. Let someone else deal with that Scirocco sister."

He wasn't sure he completely believed Owen's declaration about Blair. She had gotten under his skin, but they had a chemistry most people only dream about. The excitement might've been a bit explosive and probably what scared them both off.

"I'm catching some waves tomorrow if you want to join," Owen said.

"I'll think about it. Today was a disgrace." He wasn't sure if he was ready to embarrass himself again. Except that he had come home to figure out who he wanted to be in this life after his heart attack. Cleaning the attic wasn't going to answer that question, but maybe the waves would.

"You know that saying about getting back on the surfboard or maybe it's the horse. Either way." Owen laughed at his own joke. "And, man, ask Liv out. Tell her how you feel. It's been a long time coming." Owen slid into the truck. He pulled onto the street and honked his goodbye.

Maybe he should take a chance and convince Liv of how he felt. He had wasted enough time. The heart attack showed him that, and Owen was right too. It was time to get back on the surfboard...or maybe it really was the horse.

CHAPTER 11

The sun had set behind thick, gray clouds and extinguished the warm light from the sky. A cold, fierce wind picked up off the ocean and blew through the empty tree branches. Liv huddled into her coat and headed up Pear Street away from the beach. The house that caught fire earlier was just a few streets away. She had only wanted to pass it again on her way to the church. She wanted to give the meeting another try even though she still wasn't ready to label her situation.

A storm was scheduled to roll in and dump snow and ice on her little town sometime during the night. Snowstorms churned chunks of fear in her stomach. Whenever one happened, she found the furthest corner from any window and hunkered down with her hands shaking and sweat breaking out of every pore. Even now, she fought the bile rising in her throat.

"Stop being afraid," she said to herself. A snowstorm could not take anything more from her, but the words failed to soothe.

Each street was more deserted than the last, but she kept walking, picking up her pace so her thoughts couldn't derail her. She could use a drink to settle her nerves. Just a sip to calm her down until the storm passed. She should've stayed inside, but the desire to see the house damaged by the fire again was too strong, and she needed reassurance she didn't have a drinking problem. Five minutes at that meeting might be enough proof.

A row of overgrown boxwoods leaned into the sidewalk space, making that stretch of the street darker than the rest. The cement sidewalk was cracked and uneven. She crossed at the parked car to give herself some much-needed light that spilled from the houses and their porches. One or two homes still had their Christmas lights up even though it was January.

Her phone chirped in her pocket. She yanked off her mittens and fumbled with the phone. Aria's name lit up the screen.

"Hey, sis." She gave the boxwoods a passing glance to make sure no one crouched behind them ready to pounce. She had spent too much time in the city looking over her shoulder. No place these days seemed to offer her any comfort. No place except with Hud.

"You sound out of breath," Aria said.

"I'm taking a walk." She readjusted the phone on her ear. No one knew she had a fear of storms. She had kept that to herself all these years, too ashamed to admit it. What adult was afraid of a snowstorm? The funny thing was she would never judge one of her sisters for being afraid of anything. Aria feared the dark. She slept with a nightlight still, and Hawk always made sure the flashlights were filled with working batteries for her.

"It's freezing out, and there's a storm coming. I thought Mack gave you her car."

"You're right. She gave me her car, but I would rather walk." She should've driven tonight, but she didn't know how to handle a car in the snow. Water Course wasn't known for their excellent plowing skills. The last thing she needed was to have a wreck. Phoenix would never let her live it down.

"Where are you headed?"

She hesitated. Aria would come to some judgment, and she didn't want to hear it at the moment. The courage it took to even leave the house to come here wore her out. She had really wanted to stay at home, in the safety of a house, glued to her computer, going through the photos from earlier.

"I wanted to walk past the house that was on fire

this morning." She paused at the sidewalk in front of the house.

The house was pitch-black, but the smell of burnt wood and despair still clung in the air like a festering wound. The streetlights cast enough glow onto the lawn that the debris was still visible. It would take months for this couple to move back in, if it all. Life wasn't fair. All the planning and preparing for something, and in one split second everything they worked for was gone. Out of the control she never had.

"Don't go near it. It might not be safe. If you want to see it again for your new job, I'll ask Hawk to take you."

"I don't need any more photos. I sent Milly everything I took. Why did you call?" In the dark, the house had nothing to offer. She wasn't sure what she had hoped to see. Maybe the old woman again. Or maybe a peek inside the heart and soul of this place. It could give her insight into what Hud was going through with his house. Or better yet, what she was going through with Hud.

"I wanted to talk to you about something." Aria's voice returned her to the dark street with the bone-chilling wind blowing. She forced her feet to move again. The long shadows cast by the glow of the streetlights added to the shivers on her skin. She should get to the church before the sky opened up. She could worry about getting home in the storm later.

"Can it wait? I have another stop to make after this."

Her stomach hollowed out. Hawk must've told Aria about the meetings. She would have to confess to the extent of her drinking.

"Are you going to Hudson Lozado's house?"

"Why are you asking me that?" Had Hawk said something about seeing her at the meeting? She might still have time to decide if she even wanted her sisters to know about the drinking. She could make Hawk understand this was her journey. She wasn't hurting anyone by keeping it close to the chest. For now. Eventually, she would tell them everything. Not that there was much to say.

"You do know Hud is back in town." Aria wasn't asking a question.

"I heard." She turned off Williams Street. The church tower reached for the sky on the next block down. A swing in a child's swing set creaked in the wind. A dog barked somewhere in the distance. She hurried along.

"Have you spoken with him?"

"Why does that matter?" She wasn't ready to share her short time with Hud. She wanted it all to herself for now. Maybe forever.

He hadn't called or texted all day. He had simply walked out of the house after she fell asleep without so much as a look back. It was what she had said she wanted. She had lied. She had wanted him to stay until she fell asleep because she hated being alone at night. Her heart ached for their child at night.

She had been afraid to text him and see if he still wanted help with the attic. He may have changed his mind about wanting her around, and she didn't really want to know that.

"I just want to make sure you're okay. I don't want him upsetting you or causing you any trouble."

"He doesn't upset me." He made her remember their love and how good it was for a while. He reminded her of their lovemaking, the way he'd put his head on her belly when they would lay together so he could listen for their baby. She wanted to allow herself to give in to her feelings, but the fear of hurting again was like her hand on a scalding flame.

"But he's a reminder. A reminder I don't think you can deal with very well."

"I don't need you to babysit me. And besides, he understands how I feel." She stopped outside the church door. The short man from last time hustled past her and out of the cold.

"So do I."

"That's where you're wrong. You have no idea how I feel. I know you're only trying to help, and I guess now that you're a mom you can imagine the hurt, but let me tell you. You don't know. And I hope you never do. I don't want to talk about this anymore. Hud is none of your business."

The meeting would start soon, and she didn't want to walk in when all the folding chairs were taken. Hawk might be there again. Everywhere she turned, her pain followed her. Coming home hadn't changed a thing. Everyone held a magnifying glass up to her problems. She just wanted to forget. When was she going to forget?

"You're right. You can handle Hud, I suppose. It's been long enough. I just worry. I'm sorry. I also wanted to ask you if you've heard from Blair."

"Not in a few days. Why?"

"I hadn't either and neither has Mack. Blair's not answering her texts. I guess she's busy."

"That's probably it. You know Blair. She never sits still for long. She'll surface with some crazy story." She let out a long breath. If she didn't say something, Hawk would tattle on her. "Aria, there is something you should know."

"About Blair?"

"No, no. I really don't know anything more than you do about her. It's about me. I've started going to meetings for my drinking."

"Are you having a problem?" Aria's voice went up a few octaves. *Here comes the worry.*

"It's nothing I can't handle." She should've kept her mouth shut, but Aria had always been like a mother to her being the oldest. She could never keep a secret from her.

"Let me get Hawk. He can talk to you. Help you," Aria said.

"Wait. I saw Hawk at the last meeting. I didn't stay, though. He told me to tell you." She rushed out the words before Aria could put Hawk on the line.

"But you didn't tell me." Her words were a whisper. Aria's feelings would be hurt. She wanted the rest of them to trust her enough with all their demons.

"I am now. I don't want you to worry, okay. I just thought having someone to talk to would be nice. But I don't have a problem. I can stop at any time."

"That was what Hawk said right before he ruined our marriage the first time."

"This is different." It had to be. She had only really started drinking after the fire last year. Before that, she drank socially like most people. The fire had scared her in a way nothing else had in a long time.

"That's what they all say. Get the help, Livvie. You've needed it for a long time."

"What are you talking about?" She stamped her feet to keep the cold at bay.

"I know what an alcoholic looks like. Our father was one. I'm in love with one. And then there's you."

"I'm not an alcoholic." How many times would she have to say it before they believed her?=

"I have to go. The baby is crying."

"Aria, I don't have a problem." She didn't mean to raise her voice, but she needed her sister to understand. This was different. She was different than their father and even Hawk.

She was met with silence.

"Aria, are you still there?" She checked the screen. Aria was gone.

LIV KNOCKED on Hud's door with hands so cold she could barely make a fist. The snow fell in a horizontal white sheet and covered the ground in a thin blanket. Her insides shook and not from the cold. Bad things happened in a snowstorm. The icy roads caused accidents. People died on nights like this one.

After the meeting at the church, she didn't want to go home to that empty house where the ocean groaned on repeat and the angry wind wanted to get in. She didn't trust herself with her own thoughts all alone and all night. After listening to those people share their stories, they had dragged up too many memories for her. Memories better left alone.

Instead of walking home, she had trudged along the dark and empty streets of Water Course, convinced someone would jump out of the shadows or a car would slip on the road and crash into her. It was only her imagination, but it didn't stop her from looking over her shoulder every second.

Eventually, she found herself standing on the sidewalk outside Hud's home. The front of the house was dark. He might not be inside, or he went to sleep early. Maybe he was with a woman. She didn't want to picture him naked, screwing someone else. He had the right to take someone to bed. She just didn't want to know about it. On a long breath, she went around back and knocked.

It would've been easier to text, but he could've rejected her again. She needed to see him. She could relax around him. She had forgotten the way her body would almost melt when he was near. Nothing could hurt her. For a long time, she had believed if he had been with her when she went into labor, everything would've been okay. She had wanted to blame him because it would've been easy, but it hadn't been his fault. The snow had been more at fault than Hud.

She turned to go. He wasn't answering. She'd have to walk back in the snow and spend the night alone after all. And she would want a drink because her nerves were worn thin from the weather. Or she could call one of her sisters to come and get her, but they would find her outside Hud's. They would have lots of questions she couldn't answer.

Or she could walk to Mack's or Aria's. They weren't so far away, but she couldn't bear to see them ensconced warm and safe in their sweet families. Watching them only made her miss what she didn't have even more.

Somewhere along the way she had become bitter. She hadn't meant to. She had wanted to start over, to find her place in the world, but she had become stuck somehow. The walls she had put up to protect herself had crashed around her the minute she held that newborn. All she wanted now was to move forward.

The door whooshed open. He stood there in his sweatpants and t-shirt, smiling down at her. "You know most people stay home during a snowstorm."

"I was already out and in the neighborhood. Is it okay if I come in?" She tried to hide the desperation from her voice. She hoped he wouldn't make her go.

He rubbed his bare arms. "You were already out? Doing what?"

"Walking." Trying to get over him. Trying to learn to let her heart go. Being stupid and daring a snowstorm.

"In this weather?" His brows creased.

"Never mind. I'll go. I didn't mean to bother you." What had she been thinking? So foolish to believe he really wanted her. He had given up on her when she had forced him to. He had even gone on and gotten married. She had never done that. She had never cared about anyone enough to marry them. She had come close with Darius, but thankfully that hadn't worked out.

"Don't go. I don't want you to freeze on the walk

back. Plus, I'm glad you came over." He held the door open for her.

She ducked past him, catching a whiff of his fresh and masculine scent. She tried not to take too big of an inhale. "Were you in the middle of something?"

"I was messing with the furnace. I think it stopped working. I'm going to have to call someone in the morning to come out and fix it because I can't seem to."

She followed him up the narrow staircase that led to the family's residence. The wind continued to howl and find its way through the cracks in the old plaster.

At least he was home alone. She wouldn't have to meet some woman and explain what she was doing there.

"It might be as cold in here as it is outside." He closed the door and blocked the cold coming from the staircase and into the kitchen. "The heat makes the radiators just hot enough to keep the pipes from bursting, but not enough to warm anything up."

"Maybe try turning on the oven and leaving the door open. We used to do that as kids when my dad forgot to pay the bill." She dropped her purse on the table and shook the snow out of her hair.

"Or we can go down into the office area and light a fire. My dad's office has the old fireplace in it." He shrugged into his zip-up. She was sorry to see his biceps go. Hud was the sexiest man she had ever met, and had only gotten better with age, but he wouldn't want to complicate things between them. And sex complicated everything.

"I'd rather stay up here and be cold if that's okay."

"What are you doing here, Liv?" He followed her advice and turned on the oven, leaving the door open too.

"I...I wanted to ask you about last night." The wind screamed against the window and shook the glass in the frame. She jumped.

"It's just the wind."

"I hate storms. Especially snowstorms."

He nodded as if he understood, but she didn't ask him if snowstorms took him back to that night too, and he didn't say. He wouldn't. He would keep that to himself because his way of dealing with hurt was to push forward and not look back.

"What about last night? Do you want some coffee to warm you up?" he said.

"Sure, coffee would be great." And give her hands something to do. "I don't remember everything we said." She couldn't meet his gaze. She had tried to recall their entire encounter throughout the day, but spots were blank. She did recall bashing Phoenix some, but that had been jealousy talking.

"You were pretty wasted." He busied himself with pouring coffee into a filter.

"Was it bad?" She toyed with the belt on her coat.

"You didn't say anything to embarrass yourself, if

that's what you're worried about." He arched a brow and teased her with his wicked smile.

"What did I say?" Heat burned her face.

"You told me to get out of there. Not to bother with you." He grabbed milk from the refrigerator and placed two spoons on the table.

She dropped into the chair and shoved her hands between her thighs to keep them from shaking. "I'm sorry about that." She had remembered that too, but was hoping she was wrong.

"Forget it. I won't bother you anymore, because that's what it seems you want. What I don't understand is why you're here. You could've called or texted me about last night."

"I had to see you."

"Liv, I don't get you. You tell me you still love me. You tell me to get out of your house, and now you tell me you had to see me. You can't have it both ways." The coffee machine gurgled in agreement.

"Why did you get married?" The question wasn't what she meant to say but if she were being honest with herself, she had wanted to ask him about his marriage from the moment Mack and Aria had called to tell her. They had doubled-teamed her, hoping it would soften the blow if they were both on the other end of the phone.

She had wanted to call and yell at him not to leave her after all, that she had made a huge mistake by running away from him. She had pictured interrupting his wedding at that exact moment when guests had the chance to speak or hold their mouths shut for life. She hadn't been brave enough to show up and proclaim her love for him.

"You can't avoid the real conversation here. What do you want from me?" He leaned against the counter out of reach. She wanted to touch him the way she used to when he became serious and stoic. The way he was now.

She wasn't being fair to him. She wanted comfort from the storm and the only place she seemed to find any peace at all was with him. But she was still allowing fear to have the upper hand. She couldn't ask him to be the strength she needed without giving herself over to him.

"Did you love your wife?" She couldn't meet his gaze because she didn't want to see the truth in his eyes.

"You aren't going to answer me." He brought over the two mugs of coffee and dropped into the chair next to her. He stretched out his long legs and ran a hand over his bearded face. "If you really want to know, I thought I loved her, but now I know I didn't. And I don't think she really loved me either. She loved the idea of me."

"Was it the divorce that helped you realize you didn't love her?"

"It was probably the time I called out your name during sex." He glanced at her through his eyelashes and shrugged.

"You did not." She bit her lip to keep from laughing. A delicious, warm shiver ran over her skin. She shrugged out of her coat. Hudson had said her name during sex.

"I did. She was pissed. I can't blame her. I would've been mad too. We went downhill from there. It was inevitable. Now tell me, why are you in my kitchen at this hour during a storm? What can I do for you, Liv Scirocco?" He leaned forward, resting his arms on his thighs. His clean smell drifted toward her again.

The warmth continued to build inside her. She could easily reach over and run her fingers along his jaw, but she reached for the mug instead. "I shouldn't have sent you away last night. I'm sorry about that."

"Apology accepted."

"I would still like to help you around here."

"Okay. But you could've said all that in a text. Now, spill it."

He wasn't making this easy for her. She deserved that. She had been the one for years shoving him away. He had yelled her name outside her apartment until he was taken away in handcuffs because a neighbor complained. She hadn't even bailed him out. And now he sat opposite her, smiling that impish grin, the one he used to give her before he took her clothes off, making her sweat.

The wind howled again. She went to the window, trying to stall for time. She came here thinking she could tell him her real feelings, but she wouldn't be able to stand it if he didn't want her anymore.

The snow fell on a slant. The ground was covered with a thick blanket of it. She wouldn't be able to walk home without some effort even if she wanted to. She'd probably freeze before she even got there. Telling him how she really felt was now or never. She had put this night in play. It was time she chose bravery.

She turned to him. He watched her with interest. She had imagined this scenario a thousand times, because it had always been so hard without him. She believed in the difference between soul mates and the love of your life. The two could be the same, but not always. Hud was her soul mate. Even if he never wanted her again, and she found love with someone else, he would always be the one seared into her heart.

"I meant what I said the other night. I still love you. I always have." The words burned her throat and brought tears to her eyes.

He crossed the room in two strides and cupped her face with his hands. "I've waited a long time to hear that. You can't unsay it. If you don't mean it, then say so. I can't pretend. I can't go back. It's always been you. Always."

She laced her fingers through his and held them at her side. He was right. She couldn't go back either. And she couldn't unlove him no matter how hard she had tried. It wasn't even a choice. "I'm afraid I'll break our hearts again."

"Life doesn't come with guarantees. Our hearts might break."

She wouldn't be able to take it another time. She would jump into a bottle and never come out if she ever experienced so much pain she couldn't breathe. But maybe with Hud by her side she could stay sober and focused. She could have the kind of life she had always dreamed of because he was solid and strong. She could lean on him like a tall oak in the storm.

She wrapped her arms around his neck and kissed him. Her body lit up when he pushed her mouth open and their tongues collided. The rush of remembering all their times together washed over her like a hot waterfall. She wanted to turn her face up and drink him in because she had been denied him for so long.

The years apart washed away as if they never existed. Her hands fought the zipper of his sweatshirt until it was open, and she could shove the material to the floor. Her fingers remembered the path over his chest and down his back. She slipped her hands inside his sweatpants and cupped his butt.

He tangled his hand in her hair and tugged her head back, taking the kiss deeper. He fumbled with the button of her pants, then abandoned them to reach up her shirt. His grip on her breast was sudden and taunting. He twisted her nipple right through the fabric of her bra and drove reason right out of her head. The storm outside was no longer an issue because of the one brewing in his kitchen.

She didn't want to wait. This was urgent and desperate, as if her life depended on having him inside her.

Without breaking the kiss, he guided her backward, his hands on her backside. She leaned into him. His erection pressed into her belly. She pulled his shirt over his head and stole a second to glance at his chest.

"I want to take pictures of you." And she would at some point, but not now. Now she wanted his hands on her, driving her insane.

"Maybe later," he said between haggard breaths.

He kissed her long, hard, and deep. Her legs quivered under the desire burning inside her. She was certain she wouldn't be able to stand much longer. She wanted to feel him on top of her where she could wrap herself around him.

He returned to the button of her pants and tugged until it surrendered. He pushed her pants over her hips and moved back. "Step out of them," he said.

She pointed. "You too."

He laughed and obliged her. She had seen him naked a hundred times. More. But this time was different. He was a grown man now, no longer a young man of twenty about to become a father. He had grown into himself and wore it well. His shoulders had broadened and his waist had thickened. He had been all arms and legs once.

"I'm still waiting," he said.

She removed her pants and then the rest of her clothes. She stood before him and shivered as his gaze raked her in. A wicked grin slid over his lips. She wasn't the slightest bit cold anymore.

"Wow. You are as beautiful as ever." He took her hands. "I was going to make love to you right here on this kitchen table because I can't wait any longer, but that isn't right." He led her into his childhood bedroom. "I hope you don't mind the mattress. I wasn't expecting guests."

"The mattress is fine."

A soft white light drifted in from the snow piling up outside, giving her enough light to see. The room was different from when she was here last. The smell of fresh lemons filled the room as if he had just cleaned. The walls had been painted white and the posters that Hud had hung were all gone. The dresser where he had his trophies had been removed.

The wind continued to screech, rattling the windows. The weather was scary and dangerous. People died in storms, but she was safe. She wasn't going anywhere tonight, and she didn't want to.

She slipped beneath the comforter. The sheets were cold against her skin. "The kitchen would've been okay too." She would've made love to him anywhere.

"Not for you." He lay beside her and gathered her close. "I killed the mood a little bit by bringing us in here, didn't I?"

"Not in the slightest, but if you don't make love to me right now, I'm going to jump you. I've waited a long time for this." She pressed against him and allowed her hands to explore his back. His muscles flexed under her touch.

"I've waited a long time too. I better warn you. Things might end quickly."

"Hud, I have a confession to make." She stilled her hands.

"What's that? You have no patience for early ejaculation?"

"Shut up." She swatted him and laughed. "I don't care about that. I want you to know that every time I had sex with another man, I pictured you to get through it." She was grateful for the darkness to cover her heated face, but she wanted to be completely honest with him. No more holding back, and no more pretending she didn't need him.

He eased out of the embrace and looked down at her. The impish grin returned. "Really?"

"Don't let it go to your head too much."

133

"You never gave up on us." He ran a thumb over her bottom lip.

"No, I just gave up on me. Make love to me, please. All night. I don't want to think about the past."

He kissed her again, long, hot, and deep. His hands slid over her belly to the spot between her legs that ached for him.

Maybe it was watching that older couple earlier at the fire or really seeing what her sisters had, but she was ready to give herself over to him. They had been so good together once, before she ruined it all. Coming back to Water Course had seemed like such a bad idea, but something more powerful than she was had brought Hud into her path. That had to mean something, didn't it?

He positioned himself above her and brushed the hair away from her face. He placed soft kisses on her neck and shoulders. Many lonely nights she had wanted nothing more than to feel his touch, to smell his musky scent mingled with hers, to know she was safe in his arms. The storm couldn't touch her now.

Her insides coiled tighter each time he stroked until she would snap in half if she didn't get some release. She needed him to fill up her soul and remind her what love looked like.

"I'm ready." She gripped him and guided him to her.

"Me too." He kissed her again and entered her slowly, taking his time. The frenzy from before had cooled some, but she didn't mind. This was the way Hud made love. Deliberate. Thought out. The way he was. The thing she loved about him because she was anything but those things. He soothed her restlessness.

She wrapped her legs around his waist to feel all of him. Their movements remained slow at first. As if they had all the time in the world. She remembered their first time together. In the bedroom of his friend's house. The room had been so dark she hadn't been able to see him. Her heart had raced in her chest until she was about to burst, frightened and excited at the same time. But he had been tender and loving, checking to make sure she was okay the whole time. Holding her at the end until they both floated back to earth.

Now, her heart expanded in her chest, pressing against her lungs. She didn't think she could breathe as their bodies picked up the pace. His skin was slick against hers. She laced her fingers in his hair and kissed him.

Her body pulsed more with each second. He gripped her bottom and thrust harder as if he needed to possess her. She held onto him, afraid to let go because she could lose him all over again.

She had waited for this moment for years. Nothing compared to being loved by Hud. She placed a hand on his face so he would look at her. He gifted her a smile.

The release came with the force of the wind

outside. She let go and allowed the delicious ripples to wash over her again and again.

He called out her name and pushed up on his arms, meeting her on the other side. This time when she cried it wasn't because the wrong man was in bed with her. It was because the right one was. And now she had everything to lose all over again.

HE HELD Liv close while his body vibrated from the lovemaking. The storm continued to dump snow. Several inches must be on the ground by now, but he wasn't getting out of bed to look. The covers and her body next to his kept him warm. He twirled her curly hair around his finger.

She trembled in his embrace. At least he didn't have another heart attack in the middle of it all. That would've really scared her off. He needed to tell her about his health condition, but she might not want him once she knew he was broken. By all rights, as long as he took his meds, he'd be fine. The doctors said as much, but that didn't change the fact another heart attack could happen some time in his future. She deserved the truth so she could decide if she wanted someone like him, damaged goods.

Her tears wet his chest. He shifted so he could see her. "Hey, are you okay?"

She nodded.

"Liv, look at me." He tilted her chin, forcing her gaze up. "Did I do something wrong?"

She swiped at her face. "No way. It's not you."

"Then what is it?" He braced himself for whatever she might say, hoping it wasn't a critique of the last half hour.

"It's me and my messed-up life interfering with what was a really nice time."

Nice? "I was kind of hoping for something a little more dramatic like earth-shattering or the heavens sang."

She rewarded him with her laugh. "You've still got it, stud. If it weren't for the storm, I'm pretty sure your neighbors would've heard me screaming."

His chest swelled because the pretty lady was satisfied. "Then what gives?"

"I might have a drinking problem." She turned away from him.

"You might or you do?" He pushed up on an elbow to get a better look at her face.

"Depends on who you're asking."

"Then we'll figure it out." He tucked her close to him. Her back pressed to his front. Whatever came their way they could handle together.

"You aren't disappointed in me?"

"Not possible." He kissed her ear. Her sweet smell drifted under his nose.

"But what if I screw things up?"

"The fact that you're worried about it means you won't. If it's confession time, I have something to tell you."

She groaned. "You're not really divorced."

He choked out a laugh. "I am very divorced and at the moment very grateful. It's not that."

She turned in his arms to face him and placed a hand on his face. "What is it?"

"Very few people know this...and since we just did it and will be doing it again...I need you to know..."

"Know what, Hudson?" She narrowed her eyes.

"I had a heart attack a couple of weeks ago." Saying it hadn't hurt as much as he thought it might. He searched her face for a response.

"That's not funny." She reached for him again, but he put his hands over hers.

"It's not a joke, but just in case something doesn't work right or I start feeling weird or something, I wanted you to know."

"So I could call an ambulance?"

"You weren't going to let me die, were you?" He would rather joke with her than turn his situation into something depressing. He wanted to focus on the positive side of things and push through

"This isn't funny. We shouldn't be making jokes about something as important as your health. And why didn't you tell me before we did it? What if something had happened?"

He kissed her nose. "I didn't want to spoil the moment."

She shoved him away with another groan. "Aren't you too young to have a heart attack? Wait a second, that's why you didn't look well the other day."

He sat up and fluffed the pillows behind his back. "Are you hungry? We could whip up some eggs."

"No changing the subject. You brought it up. You can't switch gears that fast. Tell me why you had a heart attack. You're in great shape, you're in your thirties. I don't understand." She hopped out of bed and grabbed his t-shirt off the floor. "It's cold in here."

"Stay under the covers with me then."

She pointed a finger at him and remained on the other side of the room. "Start spilling."

"I was at work. I had a terrible pressure in my chest. I couldn't breathe. I broke out in a sweat, and I collapsed. The next thing I knew I was in the hospital with my boss standing over me." He threw the covers back and shoved his legs into his jeans.

"Your boss?"

"He rode in the ambulance with me. He didn't know who to call once we got to the hospital, so he stayed until I woke up."

"Did you call your dad?" She rubbed her arms. The damn house was too cold. He would get that furnace fixed first thing. For now, he dug in his suitcase for a pair of sweatpants and handed them to her.

"Eventually, but he acted the way he always does. He didn't come visit me or anything. I'd rather not tell anyone else other than you. I'm fine now. I'm on meds. I have a weird genetic condition that makes my blood thicken too much. I got it from probably the combination of my parents. If I had a child, I would want them to get tested to see if they had the gene, but I don't have to worry about that. Promise me you won't say anything to your sisters?"

"What if it happens again?" She pulled on his clothes.

"It won't. I like you in my clothes. I want to get you out of them again."

"Stay focused. How do you know you won't have another heart attack?"

"I don't, but I can't live my life like it's going to happen." That was why he had started surfing again, and why he wanted a new career. As long as Liv could accept him this way, everything else would work out.

"I can't lose you now that I have you back." She crossed the room and placed her palms on his chest. Her hands were cold, but they did nothing to chill the heat in his veins.

"You won't lose me. I promise that. You're going to have to grow old with me now. But you should also know I don't have a job either." He gathered her hands in his and tried to rub the cold out.

"So, what you're telling me is you're unhealthy with no potential? The guy most likely to succeed is unemployed and possibly broke because you probably had to give your ex-wife all your money in the divorce?"

"Something like that."

"Sign me up." She dropped a kiss on his lips.

"Seriously, I'm fine, but if we ever wanted to try and—"

"Don't say it. You're going too fast. It's only been a few hours since we even considered an us again." Her eyes grew wide, and she yanked her hands away. She crossed the room again, leaving him alone in the cold.

"I've never stopped considering an us, sweetheart. To me, it feels as if no time at all has gone by."

"I'm not the same person I was back then. You aren't either. Let's just take it slow, okay?" She paced the space between the mattress and the window.

He held up his hands. He didn't want to spook her off. This conversation could be finished another time. "Let me make us something to eat and get you more coffee."

"I hate when you do that." She crimped her hair in her hands.

"Do what?" He wanted to still her nervous habit and reassure her, but he stayed put and waited.

"Try to distract me. I mean it, Hud. We have to take

things slowly. You don't know everything about me, and when you find it out, you might not like it."

"I can handle whatever you've got." He had suspected she was drinking too much. He didn't care. He would give her whatever support she needed. He was full of flaws too. The one thing he knew to be true was when he was with her, the world made sense. That had never changed. Not for a second.

"And what if you can't accept me the way I am?"

"You just told me you have a drinking problem. Did you see me run out of here?"

"Well, no, but—"

"No buts." He couldn't take the space between them any longer and crossed the room to her. He cupped her face. "You can't scare me off, Liv. Not this time." Nothing could come between them anymore. They had already been through the worst together.

CHAPTER 12

*H*ud climbed into the attic. The storm had ended sometime during the night while Liv slept tangled up beside him. She made little noises and muttered to herself while she slept. He hadn't had a good night's sleep like that in a very long time. He planned on having many more.

He went to the window that faced east. The sun had barely slipped over the horizon yet, leaving the sky cloaked in muted grays. The day promised to be clear and cold. A fresh start, like the one he and Liv were finally going to get.

Several inches of snow covered every surface. He would have to shovel their way out later. Or he could leave them isolated in the house. He never needed to interact with the real world again. No one was looking for him. He liked it that way.

But at some point, he would have to think about getting a job. Or he could take Owen up on his offer to clean up the ocean. It was time to do something worthwhile with his life instead of moving imaginary numbers around a computer screen, making entitled people richer than they could ever imagine.

He surveyed the boxes filling up the attic. He'd start with the pile of boxes with his mother's handwriting on the outside. Those were the ones that probably had what he wanted.

The steps creaked behind him. Liv appeared in the doorway wearing his sweatpants rolled up at her ankles and a sweatshirt of his too. The clothes hung on her, but she looked adorable with her hair wild and flowing around her face. He couldn't believe how his luck had finally changed.

"Good morning." She handed him a mug. The steam from the coffee swirled in the air. "I didn't think you had any yet. You were out of bed pretty early."

"Habit. I called the furnace company. I'm on a list. Apparently, we weren't the only ones who lost heat last night. Thank you for this." He raised the cup.

"It's freezing up here and cobwebs are everywhere." She surveyed the space.

"I've made friends with the spiders." Her laughter was music to his ears. "I haven't made much progress and the company coming to clean it out will be here in a few days." Maybe the snow would slow them down too. He would be grateful for a little more time.

"I'm surprised your father kept this place so unorderly. That's not like him. He's too organized. A huge rule-follower. Like you." She smirked and sipped her coffee.

"We can't all be like you, you know." He placed a kiss on her nose so she knew he was joking.

"Rules are for suckers." She sassed him back.

She used to have a wild streak a mile long. It had been the first thing he had fallen for when he met her jumping out of the back of a pickup truck. The glint in her eye now said not much had changed.

"Memories of my mom are up here tucked away. As soon as she died, my father packed up her stuff and shoved it away. He said he couldn't look at it, but I think he just wanted to close that chapter of his life as quickly as he could."

"Everyone grieves differently."

"I guess. But it seemed so rushed. I didn't understand what his hurry was. Anyway, I'm going to save the important stuff. Do you have time to help me now?"

"Sure. I don't have anywhere to be at the moment." She put down the mug and wiped her hands.

"Start over there. Just look inside and see if anything is worth keeping. I'll start over here." He went back to the box with his name on it.

Liv's phone rang. She dug it out of the pocket in the sweatshirt. "Hey, Milly." She crossed her eyes and stuck out her tongue.

He shook his head while she listened to Milly.

"Right now? We haven't even shoveled out yet."

He walked over to her. She wrapped an arm around his waist and pressed her warmth into him.

"What is your obsession with getting photos before they even call insurance?" Liv raised her voice.

Milly's voice came through the phone, but he couldn't make it all out.

"Yes, I want my job. Fine. Yes. Fine." Liv ended the call. "I'm sorry. I have to go. There's a house over on Perry Street with a tree that fell and landed on the neighbor's house. The owners of the house already called her, giving her a heads-up about the claim. She wants me to take some photos before the tree gets moved. I have to go."

"I can drive you."

"No, it's okay. By the time you shovel the driveway, the tree could be moved. I'll walk. It's not that far. Then I can come back if you want, and if you'll let me use your computer."

"Sweetheart, you can use whatever you want." He could think of things better to use than his computer.

"I'm going to get dressed. I'll text you when I'm on my way back. Thanks for understanding." She kissed him quick on the cheek.

"This is your job. I get it." He reached for her one more time and took her mouth with his. She tasted like coffee, spicy and strong. He wanted her to have something to think about while she was working.

She broke the kiss, but smiled up at him. "You are very good at that. I won't work for Milly forever. But for now, I'd better go." She headed down the stairs to the second floor.

He went back to the box and dragged it into the sun for some extra warmth. He blew on his hands and tore off the tape that had mostly dried up.

He missed his mother all the time. She had been the one whose face lit up when he walked into the room. She had loved him unconditionally. She had been the one who encouraged him to marry Liv when they found out she was pregnant. His mother had been the one to sit him down and tell him Liv was the best thing that had ever happened to him. That she loved Liv for putting a smile on his face and helping him take life a little less serious. That he was too inside his head and Liv showed him the big world around him. His mother had wanted him to take Liv and the baby and go see the world.

His petite mother had been the one who held his six-foot frame in her arms when they lost the baby and allowed him to cry until he was spent. She told him after he was done and wiping his face with his hands that he had to take care of Liv now. His mother never judged his show of emotions that day, unlike his father.

But then just a few short months later his mother had died. He had lost her, Liv, and their son in such a short amount of time it nearly tore him apart.

"I got her back, Ma. I wish you could see it. We've got a chance now."

He pulled out a small blanket that she had knitted when she knew she was pregnant with him. The blanket was soft and warm in yellows and greens. He put it aside. Most of the items in the box were mementos of his childhood, including some of his artwork from elementary school.

She must've thought he would like to have these things someday, but he wasn't sure what he would do with it. He certainly didn't have a child to share it with. He let out a long breath. Maybe someday. He wasn't bothered by the fact that Liv wasn't ready to talk about children now. Someday they would try again. She would come around. She would make a great mother.

The last item in the box was a blue notebook. Most of the yellowed pages were blank. Halfway through the notebook his mother's scrolled writing jumped out at him. Her writing was sloped and thin. Some of the letters appeared jagged as if her hand shook while she wrote.

He grabbed the coffee and a crate to sit on. He flipped back to the spot where the words began.

His breath caught in his throat. It was a letter to him.

NOW THAT THE storm was over, the snow decorated everything with its silvery sparkle. Liv took the pictures of the tree lying on the roof of a small house. The roof was covered in snow dripping off the gutters from the sun's heat. By night, the melted snow would turn to ice and form jagged icicles. Some of the tree's long and gnarled branches had broken through a second-story window like an old intruder claiming what was his.

The two sets of neighbors wrapped in parkas, knit caps, and snow boots, argued on the lawn about whose property the tree sat on. None of them, with their angry faces and red noses, exuded anything special. They were simply four people angry with each other and angry at the world. She had seen it a hundred times before, the basic emotion of people. She couldn't create any photographic art here.

She started walking without so much as a goodbye. No one would notice she had left. They had barely noticed she was there, and she was fine with that. The snow-covered streets were quiet. A stillness hung in the atmosphere like a held breath. She walked down to the beach. The crisp, clean air cleared her head a bit.

She needed a few minutes before she went back to Hudson's. The old negative words wanted to swirl in her brain. She pushed them away with each step along the boardwalk because she had nothing to be afraid of anymore. Not even a snowstorm could hurt her now that she and Hud were back together.

Last night had been wonderful being with him. More than wonderful. She couldn't focus on life going sideways. Instead, she would concentrate on the ocean's continuous lullaby. She inhaled the salt air and let her shoulders drop.

If she were being honest, she was glad Hud's house would belong to someone else soon and not because they made love on an air mattress. Dr. Lozado's office held too many painful memories.

She didn't remember everything from that night and was honestly relieved to have some black spots. She and Dr. L had been on their way to the hospital, but the roads were impassable because of the snowstorm. The shore hardly ever saw three feet of snow because of the salt in the air, but not that night. Winter had had its way with them.

The pain had almost split her in two. She had been alone in the apartment she and Hud were renting. She had called Hud to tell him the baby was coming, but he was at school in Delaware. He couldn't take her to the hospital, but he was on his way home.

She had tried to reach her sisters to take her to the

hospital, but she couldn't reach them. Out of other options, she had called Dr. L. He had taken her to his office because his car slipped too much on the road. He said she would have the baby there. Everything was supposed to be fine.

She had expected to at least see Mrs. L's comforting smile when they arrived at the house, but she had been at her sister's. Even though Liv wanted to go to the hospital with all its equipment and fancy nursery, she didn't argue with Dr. L. She had been too frightened and unsure. Too trusting.

She remembered the pain making her scream, and the tears that came. She cried for Hud who still hadn't arrived, then Dr. L gave her something to help with the pain, but it made her drowsy. She had fought against the feeling, worried that something bad was happening, but her eyes kept closing.

Dr. L had told her to push, then stop, and push again. She couldn't recall much else before the rest of her memory went black. The next thing she knew Hud stood beside her holding her hand and fighting the tears. The antiseptic smell and the sulfur scent of blood had lingered in her nose for months afterward. She never wanted to smell that combination again.

Now, the snow-covered dunes rose up in front of her. She leaned against the cold metal fence that kept people off the beachgrass the shore needed to stop coastal erosion.

Soft music drifted on the back of the ocean's sound. She turned in its direction. A man with a beard long enough to touch the top of his coat and a cowboy hat pressed low on his head sat on a bench a few feet away. His hands were covered in woolen gloves with the fingers frayed and missing. Even from where she stood, the dirt around his fingernails was evident. His coat was old and worn in places. His feet were shoved in beat-up boots, but he strummed a guitar with skill and made music that spoke to the memories that haunted her as if he could read her mind.

She couldn't figure out how he could move his fingers to any melody in the cold, but he didn't seem affected by the temperature. His lips moved, but she couldn't hear if he was singing along or talking to himself.

She grabbed her camera and moved closer. She didn't want to disturb him or risk that he might fly away like a frightened bird. He didn't fit the typical Water Course resident in his dirty clothes and cowboy hat. He was displaced, had to be, but exactly what the small-town needed, someone with character.

She snapped some photos, making sure to get the million-dollar houses behind him. He was a contradiction to the money that lived on the ocean. He looked up then and straight at her. She froze.

He smiled and tipped his hat. She snapped him in that moment, capturing his mystery and joy at the same time. He went back to his playing as if he hadn't seen her. An electric current ran over her skin. She had something good with this one. She would put his photos with the others in her growing collection.

She enjoyed stumbling upon people's rawness. It was as if she had stumbled upon a lost treasure, and she was the only one with a key. Behind the lens she could capture a stranger's story and uncover the person they were meant to be. She had forgotten she had the ability to do that because she had made her living taking pictures of people pretending to be something they weren't.

Wasn't that what she had been doing for so long? Pretending to be someone she wasn't. She wasn't a well-known photographer for a successful magazine anymore, and she had hated that job for ages. Her art had stopped being true and honest the moment her son died and that was fifteen years ago. For all that time she had pretended she had it all under control, but she didn't.

She had drank instead. Drank to forget. Drank to pretend she didn't have a care in the world. But she had plenty of cares. She had grown up in a house with an abusive father. She had loved a man whose family was so different from hers that she had to pretend just to not lose her nerve around his father. She hadn't belonged with Hud, but now she wanted to. She didn't want to pretend anymore that she didn't love him.

Her feet hurried along the street and slipped on the snow and ice. She had to get to Hud. She had to tell him how she felt. She may have told him she loved him, but there was so much more. He was the other part of her.

Her phone vibrated in her pocket. She should ignore it. She had to tell Hud she was ready for the whole commitment, including a family if he wanted one. She could handle what the future held because she only wanted to be herself finally. Loud. Reckless. And in love.

The call ended but it immediately rang again. She dug the phone out of her coat pocket, expecting to find one of her sisters trying to track her down. Hud's name lit up the screen.

"Hey." She picked up her pace.

"I need you to come back here right away." He seemed breathless, almost nervous.

"What's the matter?" She ran faster. Hud never overreacted. He was logical and sensible. He needed all the facts before he decided how to feel. If he was desperate to reach her, something must be wrong.

"Now, Liv. Hurry. Don't stop for anything. Do you hear me? Come straight here."

"What's the matter? Are you having a heart attack?" Her worst fear was happening. She had finally found him again, and he was dying.

"I found a letter from my mother."

She skidded to a stop and tried to catch her breath. "Shit, Hud. You scared me. I thought something terrible was happening to you. Just tell me what the letter says. I'm on my way. I'll be there soon."

"No, sweetheart. I can't tell you this on the phone. Please, hurry." He cleared his throat, as if he were trying not to shed tears. "Come right in. I'm upstairs." He ended the call.

She had no idea what could be in that letter that would have him so upset. Maybe he just found out he was adopted or another man's son. That might explain some of the tension between him and his father all these years. Her heart ached for him. Whatever it was, she would be there for him. He could count on her. She slipped her phone in her pocket and ran the rest of the way.

CHAPTER 13

*L*iv let herself into Hud's house and climbed the narrow staircase once again. The place was still cold, but this time something else had settled around them. Hud sat at the folding table with an open beer and the letter next to him. He stared off into space, deep in thought, because he didn't even budge when she opened the door.

"Hud?" She eased closer.

He turned then. A small smile crept over his face, but dropped as if the weight of it was too much for his lips. "Hey. Sit down. I need to talk to you." He wiped a hand over his face and patted the chair opposite him.

"What's going on?" Her legs buckled, and she dropped into the chair. If she were taking photos right now, she would want to grab some of Hud. The pain etched deep lines around his mouth. His eyes

156

drooped with fatigue or anguish or hurt. The whites were lined with tiny red veins. Her stomach tied up in knots. She reached for the letter, but he stopped her.

"I need to tell you this first, then you can read it."

"Was your mother having an affair and you were the result?"

He stifled a laugh. "I wish it were that simple. No, sweetheart, you and me, we were lied to."

"I don't understand." And she wasn't sure she wanted to. A nagging throb built at the base of her neck and climbed into her skull. Whatever Hud had to say would change their lives, and she didn't want that. Her life had changed enough just by losing her job and coming back to Water Course. Her life had changed just last night when she and Hud made love and promised another chance to each other. She wanted to stay sober now. She didn't need to hear what he was about to say.

She jumped out of the chair. "Don't say it. Whatever it is, I don't want to hear it."

He stood too. "You need to know this."

She put her hands over her ears and squeezed her eyes shut. "No, I don't. Please don't say it." There could only be one thing he was referring to, and she couldn't imagine how they had been lied to. What was there to lie about? Had their son had some birth defect? Had she done something horrible during her pregnancy that caused the death? Had his father made a tragic mistake?

He gripped her hands in his icy-cold ones. "Look at me. My mother wrote this letter while she was sick. She needed to confess what she had found out, but she didn't know at the time."

"What? What did she know?" She groaned. Her knees wanted to give up and drop her on her butt. If Hud wasn't hanging on to her, she would have fallen. Her hands itched to grab that beer.

"My father lied. Our baby didn't die that night. He gave our son away."

"That's insane." She yanked her hands away and paced the kitchen. Her boots, wet from the snow, squeaked against the floor.

It must all be a mistake. His mother had been sick and in pain. The cancer had come up quickly, her sisters had told her. In weeks, his mother had slipped away. She couldn't have been in her right mind to imply such nonsense. Dr. L wouldn't do something like that. He wouldn't even have known how. Hud's father was even more about doing the right thing than Hud was. No. No. No. This was a big mistake. She turned to tell him so.

Hud picked up the letter and began to read. "My dearest Hudson, With only hours left of my life, I have to make a confession and hope the good Lord forgives me because I am certain you will not. I don't deserve your forgiveness, but please know, when I found out the truth, the damage had been done. I could not undo it any more than I could make the ocean be still."

She wasn't sure if she could go on listening. If she didn't make him stop, she would fall apart. "Hud, please, babe, it doesn't matter. He's gone now." Her voice trembled and betrayed her.

Hud wrapped her in a hug. She leaned into his strength and the comfort of his clean and masculine scent. "It matters. I won't read the whole thing. Just the important part. Okay?"

She nodded against his chest, afraid to speak. If Hud thought this was important, then she would trust him even if it meant destroying whatever armor she had resurrected around herself for protection. Her life was about to change even more, and she doubted it would be for the better. The tears escaped and soaked his shirt, but he didn't move. He only continued to read.

"Six months after your sweet baby left this world for the heavens above, I came upon your father on the floor in his office. At first, I thought he had fallen, but quickly I realized he was putting the floorboard back in place. Something told me not to say anything. He didn't know I was there. I watched while he rolled the carpet back over the spot and stood. His face was red as if he'd been yelling or running. His lips were white and his hands shook so much he couldn't hold the cup of coffee he reached for. The coffee spilled, and he threw the mug against the wall. I slipped away but returned to his hiding spot when he wasn't home."

"It's too much. I don't want to hear anymore." She pushed away from him.

"Liv, this is important. Our son didn't die. Do you hear me? Under those floorboards was a notebook with information about his birth. My father gave our child away to some couple."

"So, where's the notebook? Did she save it? Make a copy of it?"

"The letter said she was determined to make copies of the notebook but had to wait until my father was out of town for fear he would find her. When she finally had the chance, the notebook was gone."

"Did you look? Maybe it's still there."

"I found the spot where the floorboards were loose, but there's nothing there. Unless he hid it in the attic somewhere, but I doubt it since he didn't seem to care I was up there."

"Should we check the attic anyway?"

"We will, but I doubt we'll find anything. I would guess whatever files he had, he either destroyed or took with him when he moved out of here."

"Why would he take our child?" Her heart had been stolen that night. What kind of a monster would do something like that?

"I have no idea." He swiped at his eyes.

"Who was the couple?" She didn't want him to suffer anymore. He had lost so much too, and then she had made it worse by ending their relationship. Was he even healthy enough to withstand the stress this could cause if it were true?

"My mother couldn't remember their name. At least that's what she said in the letter, but she had tried to get my father to give her a clue. He never spoke of it. Then she got sick. She wrote the letter so we would know the truth, then hid the letter so my father wouldn't know she had told."

"Your father is the devil himself, if this is true. He's worse than my father." Her father might have been so abusive that Aria was afraid of the dark now and Mack had married a twisted man before she ended up with Phoenix, and Blair, well, Blair avoided everyone and everything, but at least her father hadn't stolen another living person.

"If this is true, our boy is somewhere. We can find him." Hud shook the letter.

"Oh, no. We can't do that." She couldn't get her head around what Hud was saying. How could their child be alive? And if he were—she couldn't breathe just thinking about the possibility—how would they find him? The whole thing was insane.

"We have to. He's ours. They kidnapped him." His eyes were black holes as if all reason had drained from inside him.

"This...this can't be happening, None of it makes sense. We should call your father. Make him explain. Your mother must've been mistaken. I mean, why not come to you then when he was still a baby? Why write in a letter and hope someday you'd find it? No, I'm sorry, Hud. I know how much you loved your mom, I did too, but the cancer must've gotten to her brain."

"You think she made it up?" He grabbed the beer and guzzled it down.

Her throat closed. She wanted that drink to steady her nerves. To help her make some sense of what was going on. She couldn't do it. Not now. Not when so much was at stake.

"Maybe not intentionally. Maybe she was confused. She saw it on a television show or something, right? I mean, your dad isn't capable of stealing our baby. And why would he do that? It was his grandchild."

"I think you're right. We need to ask him." He pulled his phone out of his pants pocket and tapped the screen.

"Wait. You think he did it?" Because once they said it, they couldn't take it back. They couldn't undo this. It would crush Hud either way. He would lose his father no matter what his father said, but this man before her would want to know the truth at all costs. He would do the right thing because that was how he was wired.

"We're going to find out."

"Let's think this through first. It's not like you to

jump before getting all the facts." The phone continued to ring.

"I'm tired of thinking it through all the time. Where the hell did that get me? I lost you because of it. I married a woman I shouldn't have because it seemed like the right thing to do at the time. I have spent the better part of my adult life in a career I hated because I thought too much. No more." He held up the phone for her to see. It was still ringing.

Her head spun. The room was suddenly too hot. She shed her coat.

"Hello?" Dr. Lozado's voice filled the kitchen. She hadn't heard him in years, but the hint of a Spanish accent was still detectable. She would remember his voice forever telling her he couldn't get to the hospital in the snow. Telling her to lie on the table and the shot would help with the pain.

Her blood turned to ice. She wanted to stop Hud from saying anything, but it was too late.

"Dad, I'm here with Liv and you're on speaker. We want to ask you something."

"Hudson, I am packing for the trip up north. I have a lot going on right now. My time is very limited. Can this wait?"

"It's important. It can't wait."

"Who are you with?" A rustling came across the line as if Dr. L was moving around.

"Liv Scirocco, Dad." Hud let out a long breath.

"I don't recognize the name. Is she a friend of yours?"

"You know Liv. The mother of my child." He shook his head and mouthed he was sorry.

The sting was small after all these years. Hud's dad hadn't exactly been thrilled when they started dating. Her family wasn't normal or respectable. Her father was abusive and most people knew something wasn't right in the Scirocco house. They had been poor, without much hope for a future. If it hadn't been for their grandfather, who had owned the bakery in town, they might not have made it at all, but he had talked to them all the time about getting an education and living a better life.

"Oh, that young lady you used to run around with. Of course, hello, Olivia."

"Christ, Dad, show some compassion for once. We didn't run around together, and you know it."

The only person who had ever called her by her given name besides a teacher on the first day of school was Dr. Lozado. He insisted on the formality and said if she was going to be a part of his son's life, then she should act with class and dignity and not go by some silly nickname given to her because her older sister couldn't pronounce Olivia.

She swallowed the knot in her throat. "Hello, Dr. Lozado."

"Dad, this is important. I need to ask you a question, and I need you to tell me the truth."

"Are you accusing me of being a liar, Hudson?"

Hud ran a hand over his face. His palm scratched against his beard. "No. Just answer the question as best you can, okay?"

"Certainly, go ahead."

"Did you give our child away?"

She held her breath. This couldn't be true. Her world was slipping right through her fingers, and she couldn't grasp any of it.

"What are you talking about?" Dr. Lozado's voice was strong and tinged with annoyance. As if Hud had no right to ask such a question. And if his mother had been mistaken, Hud didn't have any right to accuse his father of the most heinous act a person could perform.

"My son. Liv's son. The child you said died during his birth in your office. Your grandson. Did you sell him to some couple like a black-market baby?" Hud's face turned red. She placed a hand on his arm to help calm him because she didn't want him having a heart attack in the middle of this.

Dr. L barked out a laugh. "You've lost your mind. I'm a doctor with morals. I followed an oath to protect my patients. Even ones I don't care for. You're spending time with that girl again. I warned you she wasn't any good for you. She's putting crazy thoughts in your head."

Her vision blurred. She clenched her fists and stepped closer to the phone. "By girl, Dr. Lozado, do you mean me? Because I'm a grown woman now. I'm standing right next to your son, the man I love, and can hear everything you're saying. I didn't put these thoughts in Hud's head. It was your wife."

The call went dead.

CHAPTER 14

A pressure built in Hud's chest. He rubbed the spot with his fist. The pain was different from the day of the heart attack, and pain that was different was good. He hoped he could survive this new discovery because it sure as hell hurt worse than the heart attack.

"I think we should go to his house and confront him." He tossed the phone on the table and grabbed the beer. It was empty. He went to the fridge, then stopped. "Would it be better if I don't drink?"

"I can handle it."

"You sure?"

She nodded. Her cheeks were still wet with the tears she had shed. So was his shirt. Maybe telling her had been a mistake. Maybe he should've surprised his father with a visit and made him say the words to his face. The phone call had given his father a heads-up. He could be destroying any trail he may have left.

He stopped. He actually considered his mother's story to be the truth. Which meant he believed his father was capable of such a horrendous thing. Sure, he never cared for Liv, didn't want them dating, and certainly had been opposed to a marriage, but take his grandchild like a thief? But why would his mother lie about this? She never crossed her husband. What if Liv was right and his mother had made it all up? He was accusing his father without any real proof.

"I need to get to my father's house. You can stay here if you don't want to come."

Liv's hand hovered over the letter as if she touched it, she might burn. "Hud, what if...what if it's true?" Long breaths wrapped around her words.

He gathered her in his arms and inhaled her sweet scent. She snuggled against him and the pain in his chest subsided. "If it's true, then we find him, and we bring him home." He'd be damned if they would spend another minute without him.

"But he's a teenager now. He doesn't know us. Those people, if there are those people, they might be good to him. We can't..."

"We can't what?"

"I can't ruin his life by showing up in it. Look at me." She pushed away from him. "What would I have to show for myself?"

"Don't you think like that. If this letter is true, and our boy is out there somewhere, you're his mother and you're amazing. You should be with him." He wanted his son back. Their lives were stolen from them. He didn't care that he was a teenager now. He would have the rest of his life to spend it with his boy. His boy. And Liv's.

"While I was out earlier, I remembered something about that night. I hadn't really forgotten it, but in light of what we just found out I wonder if it's important." Liv grabbed a napkin and blew her nose.

"What's that?"

"When your father brought me here, he told me he'd give me something for the pain. Everything hurt so badly, and I was so scared without you I didn't even question him because women get pain meds all the time during delivery. I wanted the pain to stop. But... but the last thing I remember is pushing until I woke up and saw you." She stared at him with wide eyes. "What if he knocked me out?"

"We'll ask him that too. I'll know if he's lying." He wouldn't leave until he was certain his father was telling the truth.

"Are you going to fly there tonight?"

"I'll leave on the first plane. He's due here in a few days, but I don't want to wait. I can be back by tomorrow night. Do you want to come?"

She shook her head. "I'm going to go back to my

place and wait there. I can't stay here, and I don't want to see him. Just get him to explain it all to you. And when you know the truth, come home to me."

"If you're sure, then I'll go by myself."

She nodded. Her bottom lip trembled. She was trying to put on a brave face for him, but he knew what this was costing her because it cost him the same thing. Only she had felt more responsible because she had carried their son, and it had been her job to bring him into the world. He might kill his father for what he did to Liv.

"Sweetheart, I don't want you to be alone. Stay with me."

"If I see him, I might rip his eyes out, and I shouldn't want that because he's old now, and I don't even know if this is true. But I've already, in my head, accused and judged him because I want to believe our little boy is alive."

He dropped into the chair and hung his head. A screaming thought had knocked him off-balance. Why hadn't he considered that before?

"Hud, are you sick? Should I call nine-one-one?" Liv leaned over him. Her cold hands were on his face.

He swallowed hard because the words stuck in his throat. "If he's alive, who did we bury?"

LIV GRABBED the bottle from the top of the refrigerator where Hud had left it the other night and placed it on the kitchen table. Too close to touch it. One drink would do her in. And one drink wouldn't be enough. She hadn't touched the bottle until now because she wanted to prove she was fine, that she didn't need help, but she needed some help now.

She called Blair, but the call went to voicemail. She didn't leave a message. Blair was probably busy with her life. She tried to call Mack and Aria but stopped each time. How would she even explain this? Finding out her son was alive after all these years was something right out of a movie not real life. And what if none of it was true? Hud was on a plane ready to accuse his father of being a kidnapper and a liar. What if they were wrong?

But that shot that night. Dr. L had come toward her with a long needle and stuck it in her thigh. The room had grown fuzzy. She had reached out for Dr. L's hand because she had felt nauseous. He had said to relax. That it would all be over soon. She had expected to be holding her baby shortly after that, not finding Hud sitting in the chair beside her bed empty-handed and trying to explain to her what had happened.

Hud had wanted to be the one to tell her. He had climbed into the bed with her and held her, stroking her hair. She had cried the whole night. When she had asked to see the baby, Dr. L would not let her.

Over the years, she had avoided holding newborns. She had made an exception for her nephews and niece, but each time she had found herself huddled over a toilet vomiting afterward. That baby in the hospital recently had black hair the way she had pictured her baby would. That was why she had cradled him.

She needed to talk to Hud. Her hands shook as she dialed. Of course, the call went to voicemail. He was on a plane.

She paced as she waited for the beep. "Hud, ask him why he wouldn't let us see the baby. Ask him why, Hud. Do you hear me? Please, Hud, ask him." She hung up afraid she might start screeching.

The tears and snot streamed down her face. She couldn't breathe. She wiped her nose with the back of her hand. She couldn't stay there, and she had nowhere to go. The walls closed in on her. It would be dark soon, and she would be trapped with her thoughts. She poured the vodka into a tall glass. Just until she heard from Hud. Then she would stop.

CHAPTER 15

*H*ud banged on his father's front door. He
had taken a driving service from the
airport straight here. He wasn't leaving until he had the
entire story. He wanted to believe he would recognize
a lie, but it was likely his father had been lying to them
this whole time. He hadn't noticed the lies before. He'd
been so stupid. Why hadn't he asked more questions?
Why hadn't he demanded to see his child? His father
had preyed on their vulnerability. But why?

"Dad, open up." He shouted because he wanted the
entire neighborhood to hear him which would embarrass his father. If only he had a key, then he would just
open the damn door, but his father had never given
him one to his new place. And he had never asked.
That alone said something about their relationship.

"I'll kick the damn door down if you don't open it

173

now." He meant it. He'd break every fucking window in the house.

The door swung open. His father glared at him behind his glasses. The hair on the back of his head, more gray than black now, stuck up as if he'd been lying down. His cardigan hung on his thin shoulders, and his cheeks were sunken and sagging. For the first time in his life, his father seemed small and old. "Stop your yelling, boy, before someone calls the police. Why are you here?"

"Let me in. We need to talk."

His father stepped aside without argument and shut the door. "I was about to have dinner. Would you like some?"

The house smelled musty and dank and not of a warm meal cooking. Much the way the Victorian smelled these days. The only light on in any of the rooms was the kitchen. Every other room was left dark as a way to keep others out. The kitchen table was set for one. The napkin was folded with a crease. The way his father always wanted it. A small television played silently on the counter.

"No, thank you. I'm not hungry." He pulled the letter out of his jacket pocket. "Can you explain this?"

"Did you come all the way here to show me that? You could've sent a fax." His father spooned soup from the stovetop into a bowl and sat down.

"I needed to see your face when you read this letter. It's from Mom. She wrote it right before she died."

"Well, what does it say?" His father unfolded the napkin and placed it on his lap. His gaze kept on his task, but his father's hands seemed to shake. The movement was so subtle, Hud thought he might've imagined it.

"Dad, I told you on the phone. It says my son was taken and not dead. Taken by you. Why would she say that?" He wanted to yell at his father to look at him. For once, he didn't want to be dismissed by his father. He wasn't a child anymore. He deserved to be treated like an adult.

His father crumbled crackers into his soup. Some of the pieces fell to the table in a fine dust. "How would I know what possessed your mother to say something? I never knew what she was thinking."

"Dad, is it true?"

His father brought the spoon to his thin, chapped lips and blew on the soup. He slurped the orange liquid, ignoring the question.

He would no longer put up with his father's silent responses that meant there was nothing more to discuss. All the years as a kid, when his father had turned his back and ignored him, it meant he had lost the conversation. But not tonight after he flew fifteen hundred miles. He slammed his fist on the table. The soup jumped out of the bowl. His father finally looked at him.

"Damn it, Dad. Tell me what the fuck my mother was talking about because I swear to the God you believe in, I will do something I may regret if you don't."

His father wiped his hands on the napkin, as if this were any other conversation. "Let me see the letter."

He handed it over. His father fished his reading glasses out of his sweater pocket. When he was finished, he handed it back without a word.

"Well?"

His father stared at him for what seemed like forever. The clock on the wall ticked away the silent seconds, making him crazy. Dad pushed out of the chair and walked from the room.

He followed. "Where are you going? You can't ignore this. Do you hear me?"

"Have a seat in the kitchen, Hudson. I'll be right back." His father seemed unfazed by the letter.

Maybe his mother had been wrong. Maybe she had made it all up like Liv had said. Had he come over here with guns blazing for no good reason? He checked his phone. Liv had left a voicemail. He hit the button.

Her frantic voice came across the line. She was nearly hysterical. He shouldn't have left her alone. He should've insisted that she come along. He didn't want her to do anything stupid. He shot her a quick text.

Got your VM. I'll ask. Hang in there. It's going to be ok. I love u.

He shoved his phone in his pocket. Why hadn't his father allowed them to see the baby? He couldn't remember the reason. Some spots of that night were filled with black holes instead of clear memories. It had been months before he could think straight.

Love you. She wrote back.

He let out a long breath. She was okay. He should call one of her sisters and tell them to go over and sit with her, but he didn't have the time to explain.

His father returned holding two whiskey glasses and a bottle of Maker's Mark. "Have a seat, son." He poured two shots and handed over the glass.

"No, thank you." He wanted his head about him when he heard whatever it was his father was about to say. But he did take a seat. The whole day had worn heavy on him. He would give anything to go back in time to this morning before Liv had left and he had gone into that damn attic. But no, he wouldn't. Not if it meant his son was alive.

His dad shrugged and put the whiskey down in front of him as if he'd change his mind. Dad drank the other glass in one swallow.

"I suspected you would come here after that last phone call." He poured another and sat at the table, pushing the soup away. "From the moment your mother told me she was pregnant with you. I swore I would do everything in my power to keep you safe and give you a good life."

"Okay."

"The promise was easy to keep when you were a little boy. But once you became a young man, you had ideas for yourself different from mine. You didn't know what you were getting yourself into back then. I saw all the mistakes you were going to make as clearly as if they were happening right in front of me. I couldn't allow you to ruin all the hard work I had put into raising you."

"Ruin your work? What are you talking about?"

"You'll understand someday when you become a father."

"I was a father." In some respects, he still was. He hadn't stopped loving his boy just because he wasn't here. Every year on the anniversary he imagined what his child would look like a year older. He thought of the things his boy would be doing with his life. They would be talking about college now. Or whatever his son wanted to do because he had never planned to force him into a life that didn't fit him. Not the way his father had done to him.

It hit him then. His father's calm demeanor, sitting at the table, drinking whiskey as if nothing was wrong. His father had constantly forced the direction his life would take by saying he knew what was best. What college to go to. What to major in. Who his friends should be. His father didn't like Owen. And he sure as hell didn't want him with Liv. The pain in his chest ran down into his stomach and gripped it with two fists. He clamped his lips down so he wouldn't throw up on the floor.

"You son of a bitch. You did it, didn't you? You took him." He jumped up, knocking the chair to the ground. His vision blurred. He forced his fists to stay at his sides, because he wanted to punch his father in the face.

His father remained seated. "I told you not to get involved with that girl. She wasn't good enough for you with her drunkard father who abused those girls. What kind of a life would you have had with someone with her mental state? Mental illness doesn't go away. You deserved someone of your caliber."

"So, you took my child and lied about his death? My child." He paced the kitchen. "Your grandson."

"He was no grandson of mine. She tricked you into staying with her. She knew you had a better life waiting for you and eventually you would've figured it out. I just helped things along. I gave that boy to a couple who could never have a child of their own. You had plenty of time to have children with the right woman. You shouldn't have been tied to that woman because of one indiscretion."

"I think I'm going to be sick." He continued to force the bile down.

"Nonsense. I did you a favor. I saved your life."

"Saved? You're out of your mind. I've been tortured every single day for the past fifteen years. I lost my baby. I was in love with him from the second Liv told me she was pregnant. I had vowed, like you did, Dad, that I would take care of him and protect him for the rest of my life. I had failed him before he was even born. I blamed myself because I couldn't get home fast enough. I blamed God for sending Liv into labor three weeks early. I was supposed to be home on spring break. She was supposed to deliver then. I blamed God for the fucking snowstorm that kept me from getting up I-95 in time. I married Patricia and ended up divorced because of that night. I lost Liv, the only woman I ever loved because of that night. So, fuck you, old man. The last thing you did was save me from anything."

"Sit down and have a drink. You'll see in time it was all for the best. And if you are so determined to be with that wretched woman, then have another child with her. You're both still young enough."

He flew across the room and knocked the whiskey glass out of his father's hand. He gripped his father by the fabric of the cardigan and lifted him out of the chair. His father stared in disbelief. His mouth hung open. White spit formed in the corner of his lips.

"You are going to tell me who that couple was. Do you hear me? You will give me every piece of information you have on them before I leave here. Then you and I are through. I will never speak to you again." He dropped his father back in the chair.

"You're upset right now."

"You're damn right I'm upset. My own father. How could you? How could you hurt me so badly? Did you ever really love me at all?" The tears stung the back of his eyes, but he would not cry in front of this man. His father always saw tears as weak; he wouldn't give him the satisfaction. He would go home to Liv and cry with her.

Home. Where was that? He couldn't stay at the Victorian. He would not help his father anymore.

"Everything I've done for you is because I love you. I have always had your best interests at heart. I wouldn't have taken matters into my own hands if I hadn't felt so strongly about it."

"You're not even sorry."

"I'm sorry you feel sad, but you should be sorry too. You hurt me by dating that girl when you knew I didn't like her."

"Who did you give him to?" He couldn't even acknowledge the nonsense his father was spilling. He had nothing to be sorry about except the fact he never saw this coming. In his wildest dreams, he could not have imagined his father was the devil himself.

All the years he had tried to please his father by doing what he was told had all been for nothing. He had wasted his entire life trying to make his father happy. He wanted to scream.

"I don't know their real names."

"How did you find them? Did you have this planned all along?"

His father stared at him.

"Say something. You owe me the whole story, and you know it."

His father picked up the whiskey glass and rinsed it at the sink. He poured another but didn't offer him any this time. "I had thought about it many times during the pregnancy, but no plan formed until Olivia called me about being in labor. I knew before I went to her the roads to the hospital were impassable. I brought her to the office. Everything else just fell into place."

His beautiful Liv had been frightened out of her mind when her water broke. She had called him crying because it was too early and the snow was coming down in sheets. The pain had already started by then, and she was all alone. He had told her to call his father. How stupid he had been. He thought he was helping her.

"I still don't understand how you found them." He would hunt this couple down if it were the last thing he ever did. They were going to give back his son.

His father sipped his drink. "A colleague of mine often helped couples who weren't suitable for the public adoption list. You know, older couples or homosexual couples. Teenage girls like to give their children to people who look like them. That rules out many. I called him before I went to Olivia's house. He set it up. They met me at the back of the house before you arrived from school."

"That's why you wouldn't let us see the baby. He was already on his way with that couple." At least he had something to tell Liv now. It would kill her to know the truth. It was killing him.

"I certainly couldn't produce a stillborn for you to hold on to," his father said as if this made all the sense in the world.

"Who did we bury, Dad?"

"Why does that matter? I gave you a chance to grieve and get on with your life, but I can see you didn't do that. How did you find that letter?"

"You had no idea that letter existed, did you?" He had to assume if his father had any idea the letter was somewhere in the house, the house would've been set on fire before he could get his hands on the message from his mother.

"Certainly not."

"Tell me who the child was we held a funeral for."

"If you insist on knowing all the details, fine, but none of it matters now. A child had been left outside the state hospital in the snow in the middle of the night. By the time someone found him, he had frozen to death. No one had come to claim him. You did that child a favor. He would've been buried in a nameless grave."

"You've committed a crime. You and your friend and that couple. I want the names they gave you. And if you don't tell me right the fuck now, I'm going to call the police and have you arrested."

His father stood and glared at him for the first time. Being arrested was the thing that had him moving. He did not want to risk his reputation. That mattered above all else.

His father left the room. He leaned against the counter to catch his breath. How was he going to repeat all of this to Liv? He might not be able to get through it a second time, but he would do whatever it took to find their child and bring him home. Those people had stolen him.

"Here." His father returned with an old pocket-size notebook. "Their names are in it, but it won't do you any good to know what they were. You can't undo it now."

He flipped open the book. The names were there, but no phone number. Dad had documented the size and weight of their son and the time of his birth. He ran his fingers over the numbers. His father had included a description of the couple's car and their license plate, as well.

"Why did you write down what kind of car they drove?"

His father shrugged and poured another whiskey. His hands shook while he brought the glass to his lips.

"Why?"

"I don't know. It seemed important at the time."

"Was it in case this ever happened? That Liv and I found you out? You would have one small detail to give us so we could find them?"

"I don't know. You have what you want. Go now. Get on with your life."

"I'm moving out of the Victorian as soon as I get back. I won't bother cleaning out the attic any further."

"I supposed as much."

"Goodbye, Dad."

"Good luck, Hudson."

CHAPTER 16

Someone banged on the door. Liv didn't move from her place on the couch. If she did, she might come unglued. Sitting perfectly still since she had received Hud's last text had been the only thing to keep her sane. She hadn't moved in hours.

She had played a game with herself at first. How long could she go without moving? Not a muscle. She hadn't even blinked. Then how many breaths could she count without thinking about drinking. Now, she was afraid to do anything except breathe.

"Liv, it's me. Can you open the door?" Hud's muffled voice came through the wood. He would continue to knock until she answered. She didn't want him to worry about her any more than he might already be. That last voicemail she had left for him had her sounding like a crazy person.

She stood as if she were an old woman made of glass. With each step, her joints remembered how to work a little more. She opened the door to Hud standing there with his suitcase and his duffel bag over his shoulder. A rose-colored flush covered his cheeks. But the dark circles under his eyes had her worried.

"It's worse than I thought," she said.

He brushed past her and brought a cold breeze with him. "I can't live there anymore. Can I stay with you for now?"

"You can stay with me forever. We'll have to ask Mack how long she'll let us camp out here. They're going to want to come back after Phoenix's house sells." She closed the door and locked it, not because they weren't safe in Water Course, but because she wanted to keep the demons outside. The joke was the demons were everywhere she was.

He dumped the bags in the corner and shrugged out of his coat. He looked at the vodka on the coffee table, then back at her. "Are you okay?"

She dumped the full glass into the sink and what remained of the bottle. He was always worried about her. She had been a fool to ever let him go.

"I didn't touch a sip. Believe me I wanted to drown inside that bottle. But I kept thinking about you at your dad's finding stuff out. The longer you were there, the more I knew whatever you were learning was bad. Really bad. I had to stay strong for you. If you could sit there and take in all that information by yourself, you were going to need me after. I wasn't going to let you down again. Or ever."

He gathered her in his arms, and she pressed against him. He smelled like clean cotton and salt air. She wrapped her arms around his middle and drank in his strength instead of the booze.

"We have a lot to talk about." He ran his hands over her hair. His gentle touch soothed the prickliness in her skin.

"Will I be able to handle it?" She prayed she would be able to take whatever he had to say. Once she heard it, she would never be able to unknow it, and right about now, not knowing the whole story would keep her safe, but she couldn't play it safe forever. At some point, she'd have to face the truth.

"We'll handle it together. Let's sit. I'm exhausted." He held her hands and pulled her to the couch.

"I'm afraid, Hud." She blinked away the tears threatening to come and focused on his face. As long as she kept him in her sights, she could do this.

"Me too. Promise me one thing?"

"Sure."

"Promise me no matter how bad this gets, we stick it out together. Then afterward, if you don't want to be with me, or if you don't love me anymore, I'll understand. I'll leave you alone. I just can't get through this without you."

Her heart broke in two. Her sweet Hudson. What had she done to him all these years? She had been so selfish. "I'm not going anywhere unless you tell me to. I was wrong to break us up. I have always loved you and always will. Always."

"Always," he said on a long breath. "I'm trying not to fall apart. Please be patient with me."

"Never be sorry for being transparent with me. You've learned about my ugly side."

"I don't want you to think any less of me if I handle this badly."

"You're entitled to have a tough time with this. We've been robbed of our child regardless of what you're about to tell me. I promise never to break your heart again. You are the strongest man I know. Seeing you upset doesn't change that for me. In fact, if you need to get more upset, that's okay too."

She wanted him to know it was okay to cry if he needed to. It wasn't like him to show all his emotions. Even when she had woken up and saw him in the room with tears in his eyes, he only cried while he told her what happened. When his father had walked back in the room, Hud had pulled himself together.

"I want to take care of our problem before I let my emotions get the best of me. I need to keep my head about me. We're about to be in the fight of our lives."

"I know what you have to say is important. I can guess the worst of it. He's alive and out in the world somewhere growing up without us. But can you hold the details for a little while?"

"Why?"

"Would you make love to me instead? I want to love you one more time before I know it all. Before every sordid detail worms its way into my mind and takes root there. It could be a while before we make love again after that. I want to hang on to the good stuff while we work through the bad."

"Are you saying after I tell you, you won't love me anymore?"

"Not at all. I meant what I just said. I will always love you. I want you in my life forever. But I don't want all my memories of our lovemaking to be colored by the details. Does that make any sense?"

"I'm not sure, but I don't care if it does. All I want right now is to love you and hold you and know you're mine. The details can wait until morning."

She led him to the bedroom. He cupped her face and brought his lips to hers. His touch was soft at first, but then he tangled his hands in her hair and gave a tug. She moaned against his mouth. Her hands went up his shirt and ran over the lines and plains of his chest. The cotton was in her way. She wanted nothing but skin against skin. She tugged his shirt above his head, breaking the kiss only long enough to discard it, then removed her own shirt and bra.

He fought the button of her jeans until it popped

open and shoved them down her legs. She undid his belt and zipper and freed him. He pulled her to the bed, not bothering with the moving the covers.

Their kisses were savage and messy. She wanted to taste all of him and bit his lip in a playful tug. He growled low and guttural. He took her chin in his hand and consumed her mouth, driving her mad. He ran his tongue down her neck and nipped at her collarbone. He took her breast in his mouth. His teeth grazed her skin and sent painful pleasure over her body. She held his head against her, not wanting him to stop.

His hands possessed her, touching every part of her with an urgency. She craved the frenzy. She needed to feel as if she were the only other person in the world for him because he was that for her. She wanted his hands on every part of her, claiming her. She moved her hands all over him defining what was hers now and forever.

She stroked him. He stilled her hand. "Not yet."

"I want to touch you." She brushed wisps of hair off his damp forehead.

"I won't last."

"Then no more foreplay."

"Are you sure?" His smile spread across his face.

"Never more." She gripped him and placed him at her entrance.

He thrust inside her, and she let out a long breath. The feel of him inside her was what she had wanted.

He filled her up like the swell of the ocean. She rocked her hips to the rhythm he set, rising up to meet him thrust for thrust. Their movements were quick and hard. His fingers bit into her bottom as he pulled her closer.

The ache between her legs drew her higher and higher. She couldn't stand the tugging inside her another second and never wanted it to stop either. He looked at her and smiled. She kissed his face and let everything go.

Her body gave way to the release. Ripples of delicious pleasure poured over her. She shivered against them and held him closer. Her muscles gripped him with each shock of the wave that hit her.

He buried his face in her neck. "God, Liv. Being with you is amazing," he said and met her on the other side of the crash.

SHE CURLED against Hud and relished his warmth. Her body began to cool down from their sweaty lovemaking. She rested her head on his chest and enjoyed the pounding rhythm of his heart, but then stopped.

"Are you okay?" She hadn't bothered to ask him if sex was bad for him. She had been so caught up in the way her body responded to his, reason had left her brain.

"Perfect." His voice held a dreamy quality.

"But your heart, we didn't do any damage, did we?" She shifted to see his face better. A devilish smile played across his face.

He laughed. "Think of sex like working out. The more we do it, the better."

"I'm game for that." She snuggled against him again and pulled the blanket at the end of the bed over them. "I wish we could stay like this forever." But they would have to go back to the real world soon, and everything would change. She wouldn't be afraid with him this time. Not anymore. She had given her whole self to him, and he hadn't hurt her.

"Me too, but we're going to have to figure out our next move."

"I don't want to look for him. I don't want to mess up his life." She had thought about that while Hud was at his father's. She wasn't the kind of person someone would be proud to have as a mother. Not yet anyway. Maybe someday. She hoped their child had a good life and was happy not knowing who his birth parents were.

"But he's ours. He was stolen from us. Those people should be arrested." He pushed out of bed and paced the room, confident in his nakedness.

"Then your father would have to be as well." She gathered the blanket around her even though Hud had just had his hands all over her. Talking about their son made her insecurities rise to the surface like spoiled milk in hot coffee.

"I know. I don't care. He took our boy from us. We were robbed of watching him grow up. He should've been with his parents, not some strangers." He shoved his legs into his boxer-briefs and sat on the corner of the bed with his head in his hands.

"They aren't strangers anymore." She sat beside him. Her shoulder pressed against his.

"They weren't supposed to have him." He wiped a hand over his face. "My own father hated me so much he took my child from me."

"I can't believe I'm about to defend him, but he doesn't hate you. He did it because he loves you and in his twisted way, he thinks he helped you. It's me he hates." The words tasted like sawdust, but they were true.

Hud turned to face her. "He's a bastard and stupid. You are the very best thing to happen to me. I've never been happier than when I'm with you. I can be myself when I'm with you. You accept me exactly how I am."

She had been the lucky one. He had had a future she could only dream about, and not only had he fallen for her, he had wanted to include her in his future. "You make loving you easy. You always put me first. I hope I don't let you down through this. I've been selfish most of my life."

"You aren't selfish. The opposite. You care too

much, and that's been as much of a problem for you. You thought you disappointed me when we lost him. You tried to spare my feelings by leaving me, by giving me a chance to move on without the constant reminder every time I looked at you."

"But I didn't let you have a say. I just ended it." And she hadn't been completely honest with him. She had told him she needed space, that in time they would get back together. When she had walked away from him that night, she knew she wouldn't come back. The only thing she hadn't lied about was loving him.

"Let's leave the past in the past, okay?" He brushed a hair away from her face. His touch was soft and sent a flush over her skin. She wanted to climb back under the covers with him and make love to him all over again.

"Okay."

"I want to figure out how to find our son." The glare in his eye and the set jaw said his mind was made up.

"What are we going to do if we find him? Are we going to knock on the door and say, 'hi, we're your real parents'? If he's happy, I want to leave him alone. I don't want to upset him."

"I want my son back."

She didn't think she could show up in this boy's life and destroy it, not if he was happy. Maybe these parents were good to him. Maybe they didn't even know how they came to get him. She and Hud would be destroying lives if they tried to get him back.

"Hudson, what if he doesn't want to come with us?"

He tapped her thigh with his finger. "But he's ours."

"Imagine how frightened he might be if we turn his world upside down and bring him back here where he knows no one and nothing. What kind of parents would that make us?"

"Not a day goes by that I don't think about him." His words were a whisper.

"Me too, and I'm so sorry this happened, but he's a teenager now. He might not even know he's adopted."

"But what if he does? Maybe he's curious about his birth parents. He might have questions like does he look like us. Or maybe he has your creative side and wants to know if either of us do too." Hope filled his eyes, and her heart broke. Hud wasn't used to a life filled with disappointments, but she had learned not to expect too much because it was almost always taken away.

"I know finding out our child was stolen isn't fair. I would give anything to see him or even to touch him, but I don't want to destroy him." Not hurting him was the only thing she had left to give her boy.

"I can't believe you don't want to find him. I thought for sure you'd be the one dragging me along." He narrowed his eyes.

"I do want to find him. But I keep thinking about

what it will do to him if he finds out he isn't who he thinks he is. Leaving him alone might be the one good thing I can do for him."

"I don't agree. He's ours. He was taken from us. They have no right to him. They don't deserve to have him in their lives." He punched his leg.

"What if he has siblings? Friends at school? A girlfriend?"

"I don't care. Shit, I do care. I don't know what to do." He fisted his hands in his hair.

She took his hand and entwined their fingers. For a second she couldn't tell where she left off and he began. He was the piece of her that had been missing for so long. "Maybe we should consider leaving well enough alone."

"I don't know if I can agree to that. What if he has a bad life? What if they're awful to him?" He jumped up and ran a hand over his face. "Liv, we have to find him. I'm begging you to do this with me."

"Hud, please. I need more time to think about it." At the very least, she wanted to be dressed when she made her decision. This was the most important thing she would ever do. For some reason she associated clothes with being adult enough to decide.

"We have to find him. He has to be told about my heart condition. It's genetic. He could have it too. He needs to know so the doctors can watch it. It's the right thing to do."

She had a hard time arguing with that point. Anyone would want to be aware of a life-threatening genetic condition that could show itself at any point. "Okay. We look for him, but if it's only about your health condition, then we contact the parents first. We let them decide what's best."

"Liv, he's still ours."

"Promise me, Hud. We take this slow. We think it through first."

"Of course. Of course. What else would I do?"

Any other time she would have no doubt. But this... this was something very different. Hud might be a thinker, but he was also determined to succeed. And that little character trait scared the hell out of her at the moment.

CHAPTER 17

*T*he house was full of people. All those bodies around the living room sitting on the couch, the chair, and the floor created too much heat. Sweat dripped down Liv's back as she stared into Mack's, Aria's, Phoenix's, Hawk's, and Owen's shocked gazes. She had wanted Blair there too, but she still wasn't answering her calls or texts. Liv was beginning to worry about Blair, but Mack swore she'd get ahold of her.

Liv grabbed Hud's strong hand for support. He smiled down at her and her frayed nerves mended. She wanted to kiss him for being her anchor through all of this, but she would spare making him a display in front of their families. Later, when they were alone, she would show him how much she appreciated him.

"We wanted you all here so we could tell the story

once and answer your questions the best way we can," Hud said.

Her heart rattled around in her chest like a loose screw. No one said anything. "Not even a wow or holy shit from one of you?" she said.

"I don't know what to say." Mack pulled her hair from the tie, then put it right back up.

"I'll say it. Holy shit." Owen grabbed his beer. "What can we do to help?"

"I don't think you should do anything," Aria said. "You don't even know if you can even find him. And if you do, how are you going to handle it, Liv, if he rejects you?"

"I'll worry about that later." She hadn't wanted to think that far ahead. If they did find him, and he refused to meet them or hated them for giving him up, or anything bad at all, she was worried it would be the end of her. Hud had promised to be by her side and keep her from being destructive, but what if he couldn't handle her falling apart?

"I think you should worry about that now. It's a possibility that he won't want to know you. And I know you. You will go to pieces," Aria said.

"I'll be fine." So much for the support from her oldest sister.

"Oh, come on. Your boyfriend broke up with you, and you dumped a bowl full of punch on his head at a work gala in front of hundreds of people. Then you went on a drinking bender. What are you going to do if your child rejects you? Someone with your problems can't handle that much hurt. Hawk, help me out here." Aria turned to her husband for solidarity.

Hawk leaned against the wall in the corner next to the fireplace. He put his hands up. His eyes grew wide. "Don't put me in the middle."

"But you understand better than anyone what can happen when something tragic strikes," Aria said.

"Oh, boy," Phoenix said from the other corner. Mack shot him a look that shut him up.

Hawk pushed off the wall. "Aria, you're putting me in a bad spot. Sure, everyone here knows about my past and that I'm an alcoholic. But I don't have any idea how Liv and Hud feel right now. If your sister says she can handle it, then believe her. You don't need to protect her."

She wasn't expecting so much from Hawk. He rarely spoke that much in a big group. "Thank you," she said.

He nodded.

Aria glared at her husband.

"Aria, don't be mad at Hawk," Mack said. "I agree with him. Liv knows herself. We're here for you. Whatever it takes, you can count on me and Phoenix. I want to know my nephew."

She fought the tears bubbling up. Having Mack on her side made whatever they had to do a little easier to face. She needed the support of the people she loved.

"Do what you want, Liv. But don't say I didn't warn you if this goes south." Aria untangled her crossed legs from her spot on the floor and walked out.

Hawk let out a long breath. "I'll talk to her. Listen, like Owen said. If you need any help, let me know." Hawk followed the path Aria took.

She had wanted all of her sisters on her side, but if Aria couldn't understand how much this meant to her, then there was nothing she could do about it now. She had hoped, as a mother, Aria would understand, but it had always been Aria's job to protect them from hurt. She was still doing it even though she didn't have to anymore.

"I'm due at the firehouse." Phoenix checked his watch. "I'm sorry for what you two are going through, but like Mack said. Whatever you need. I can make some calls to the police department. I know a few detectives on the squad."

"Thanks. That means a lot to me," she said.

Phoenix gazed at the floor, then back at her. "Look, I know we don't always get along, but we're family. Family always comes first. Hud, I'll call you."

"He's my ride." Mack folded her in a big hug. She smelled like sugar and cookies. "I'll call you later. You're doing the right thing."

"Thank you. It means a lot to me that you support us." An errant tear slipped out and ran down her face.

Mack wiped the tear away the way she had so many times when she was little. She would never have survived her childhood without her sisters. "I only want you to be happy. You deserve that." Mack turned to Hud. "Keep that smile on my sister's face. I know you can't control what happens with your son, but don't break her heart."

"You don't have to worry, Mack. She's safe with me." Hud grabbed her hand and kissed her knuckles. His hungry gaze never left hers.

"I didn't mean seduce her right in front of me. Gross," Mack said on a laugh and followed Phoenix out the door.

She dropped onto the couch and fought the urge to pour a drink even after Mack just said exactly what she needed to hear. All of this was too much, especially Aria not understanding and Blair disappearing, but her life now would always be her wanting a drink, but never having one.

Owen pushed out of the chair. "Phoenix might have some contacts at the police station, but my friend, Chase Shepherd, works for a special investigative team with the best technology, tactics, and contacts. He's ex-military and got involved with top-notch security after he served. Give me what you know about this couple. I'll ask him to look into it."

"Thanks, man." Hud shook Owen's hand. "I'll pay whatever your friend costs."

"No way. Chase probably won't even charge me, but if he does, I'll take care of it."

"I can't let you do that. This is our problem."

"That's where you're wrong. You're family. You and Livvie."

Owen and Hud had been friends since grade school. Owen had been the playful side of Hud's serious coin. But Owen wasn't just talking about his friendship with Hud. Owen had loved Blair once, and Blair had loved him back, but they couldn't make it. She always believed Owen and Blair would get married, but it seemed the Scirocco girls learned love the hard way.

"Owen, I won't let you pay my debts." Hud's jaw twitched. She almost jumped up and got in the middle, but both of their prides were in play. She stayed in her spot on the couch.

"Yeah, you will. Cause you're coming with me to Hawaii to clean a beach. But after you find your son. I'm sorry about what your dad did. Maybe you should use Phoenix's guy to send your dad to jail."

"I'm thinking about it."

"Livvie," Owen said. She pulled her gaze to meet his. "We'll find him. Text me that info. And I'll be in touch." Owen grabbed his jacket and left.

The house echoed with the silence. She was suddenly cold and pulled the blanket on the couch over her shoulders. Hud sat beside her and stretched out his legs. He leaned his head back on the pillows, staring up at the ceiling. "You okay?"

"I don't understand Aria." She had expected Aria to be the first one to take up arms in this fight. Aria had always been the one to come to her defense when something went wrong. Aria had always stood up to their dad when he came after her. She had learned to depend on her big sister during those scary years.

"She's trying to keep you safe." Hud grabbed her hand and squeezed it. "I can understand wanting to protect you. I want to do it too."

"Just being with you is the thing that keeps me protected. Aria thinks I'll fall apart and ruin my life because I can't handle when something goes wrong. But that isn't going to happen again. I have too much to stay sober for now."

"Aria wants to keep you from feeling heartache."

"No one can stop that. Besides, I've already experienced the worst kind of heartache. I thought he was dead. Back then, I wasn't even sure if I wanted to go on without him. Finding out he's out there somewhere doesn't hurt the way I thought it might." She had expected to dissolve into a puddle, unable to move, but once she found out the truth, the one thing she really wanted was to keep her boy safe. He needed that from her now.

"It's been her job to take care of all of you. She

doesn't always know how to turn that off. She has a point, though. He might reject us. I've pushed you into finding him. I don't want you to hate me if hunting him down backfires." Hud gathered her in his arms. She snuggled against him, relishing his warmth and clean scent.

"I would never hate you. I never have. No matter what happens, you and I will still have each other." She could never change how she felt about Hud. He was her life force, and she had been a fool trying to run from it most of her life. "He needs to know about your heart condition."

"A letter or email could take care of that. We don't have to show up at his door." He twirled his fingers through her hair and sent a heady current over her skin.

"A letter or email wouldn't be enough. Even if we don't try to take him back, we have the right to see him. I want to see our boy. Even if that's it. I want to be able to look at him as he is now since I never had the chance to see him as a baby." Tears tried to steal her breath, but she fought them.

Hud shifted so they faced each other. The dark circles had returned and hung low like a pregnant moon. He hadn't slept much the night before. She had woken in the early hours to find him on the back porch staring off into the distance.

"I never told you about the other baby," he said.

"Hud, this has been a long day for both of us. You can tell me later. You look like you need to rest."

"You don't have to worry about me. I'm okay. I promise. You need to hear this."

She let out a long breath. He was stronger than she was. She was ready to forget the day, but in the past that would have meant a few glasses of wine or vodka. Instead, she stood and tugged him to his feet. "Let's go for a walk. The fresh air will do me some good."

They grabbed their coats and walked to the boardwalk. The cold air snapped against her skin. Stars filled the black velvet sky. The ocean greeted them with its lulling sound. She inhaled and let the salt air fill her lungs and clear her head some.

She laced her fingers through his as they walked. The lights from the nearby town flickered in the distance. They were the only two people out. She liked having the boardwalk and the beach to themselves so they could work through this mess untouched by anyone.

"Do we need to find the parents of the baby we buried?" How many more people were hurt by what Dr. Lozado had done? And all because he didn't like her. It was easy to believe the bad stuff about herself because too many people had told her she wasn't worth it. She wouldn't believe them any longer.

"He was abandoned outside the hospital. No one

claimed him. They had discarded him like trash." Hud kept his gaze ahead, but the twitch in his jaw was back.

How desperate does someone have to be to do something so heinous? An innocent child had no way to fight against the brutality of an adult. She and her sisters knew that better than anyone. It was really only by luck they had all survived. Knowing the pain of abandonment was one of the things that had driven her to pick up that newborn a few weeks ago.

"Well, if there was anything good to come from this, at least we gave that boy a decent burial," she said.

"But he has our name on his stone." Hud led her to a bench. He didn't sit, instead he leaned on the rails of the metal fence.

Our name. Her heart expanded until it filled her throat. "That's okay. If he was abandoned, he needed a name. I can't think of a better one than Lozado. You gave him a gift by making him part of our family." The tears spilled freely down her face. She loved this man so much it hurt. He gave his love away without asking for anything in return, and then went on to think he might not be good enough to share his name with a stranger.

"What did I ever do to deserve you?" He sat beside her and wiped the tears from her face.

"I think it's the other way around." She wrapped her arms around his neck and pulled him in for a kiss. His lips were cold, but the kiss was hot.

"When we find our boy, I want him to look like you." He dropped his forehead to hers.

"I bet he looks just like you did at that age." She pictured a tall boy with Hud's dark good looks. Hud had been six-foot tall by the time they were sixteen. She would look for him coming down the hallway at school. He stood a head taller than most of the other kids. She could always find him in the crowd, and she would smile, because he had been hers. They had belonged together. A real family.

The tears stuck in her throat again. She might be doing a lot of crying in the coming days. She cupped his face to hold his gaze. His beard tickled her fingers. "I love you."

"Always, sweetheart. Always." He kissed her again.

"Now what?" She stood and stretched like a languorous cat in the sun.

"We take Owen up on his offer. I'll send him the information we have." They resumed their walk, turning toward the direction they had come.

A silence settled between them. Hud shoved his hands in his pockets and stared straight ahead. His jaw twitched under that beard.

"What are you thinking about?" Maybe he needed to distract some of the thoughts in his head.

He turned to her and blinked as if he were returning from somewhere far away. "What would you say if I went with Owen for a couple of weeks?"

"To work with him?" They turned onto their street.

"Yeah." He stopped on the front walk. A car drove past.

"If that's what you want to do." She would never stop him from seeking the things he wanted. She had no right to anyway.

"I'm going to need a job, and I want to do something that makes a difference for a change. I've always admired what he did and wished I had followed some of my dreams the way he had."

"Will you be happy cleaning beaches? It's noble, and you'd have fun with him, but you never mentioned wanting to do what he does."

"I think spending some time helping people would be good for me instead of making money for people who don't need any more money. I've been lost for a while. The heart attack just made me take a hard look at myself." He unlocked the front door and allowed her to enter first.

He tossed his coat on the sofa and began gathering kindling in the basket by the fireplace. "It's cold in here now."

She wasn't cold, but he needed something to do. He wasn't happy unless he was moving. He hadn't said it in the exact words, but the heart attack had scared him. She wanted to erase the crease between his brows. If working beside Owen was the way to do that, then he needed to go. She would be there when he got back.

"The fire will be nice." She shrugged out of her coat too.

He smiled at her over his shoulder, but the circles had returned under his eyes. She wanted to comfort him, bring him peace. If fighting for their son would do that for Hud, then she would stand beside him.

"I know you don't want to take pictures for Milly forever." He stood and wiped his hands on his pants.

When her boss had fired her, she hadn't really been surprised. She had been mad at herself for not quitting sooner. She had known for a long time that her job wasn't filling her up anymore. She wanted to make art. That was why the pictures she'd been taking of people around town had fulfilled her more. She wanted to capture real life. She even had some ideas for a compilation of photos of people down at the shore. Maybe even a series of pictures of locals and tourists at the small ice cream shop eating ice cream. She wanted to compare flavor choice to personalities. Or something weird like that.

"I totally forgot." She smacked her head. "She sent a text a while ago. There was an accident out on Route Thirty-Five. I have to go out there and take some photos. Will you be okay here alone?" She grabbed her coat again and her purse. Milly would kill her for taking so long to get to the accident site.

The last thing she wanted to do was leave Hud now.

She had had enough of reality recently to last her a lifetime.

"I don't have anywhere else to be." He shrugged with that impish grin. "I'll start dinner."

She cupped his face. "I don't know how I got so lucky. When I came back to town, I was so jealous of my sisters and their relationships. Today when you stood beside me and held my hand when we told that story, I knew I could do anything because I had your love."

He kissed her long and deep. She wrapped her arms around his neck and wanted to turn off the rest of the world. Just her and Hud hunkered down in this little house, making love all night. She didn't allow her hands to roam where they wanted to. She eased out of the kiss with regret.

"I have to go to work. Let's pick this back up when I come back."

"Deal." He ran a thumb along her lip.

She grabbed her camera and headed out to the accident.

MOST OF THE accident was cleaned up when she arrived. Milly would be pissed that she hadn't snapped a few photos of both cars. She still shook her head at Milly's strange insistence to photograph the damage before the claim was put in, but if a client called her or the chief of police who was part of Milly's bridge club, then Milly wanted someone to run out there, and that someone was Liv. This crazy job did give her a paycheck, and she was grateful for that. She had to support herself. Hud didn't need to do that for her. He did enough for her just loving her.

Only one car remained at the site and was lifted onto the back of a flatbed tow truck. The yellow spinning lights of the truck reflected the glistening glass and metal in the street.

She turned to go, unable to get a good shot of anything, but stopped in her tracks. A woman and boy, around fifteen maybe, huddled together on the side of the road. They watched as the battered car rose on the truck as if it were a body bag slipping into a hearse. The boy leaned his head against the woman's shoulder. His face contorted with anguish. She wrapped an arm around his shoulder and pulled him closer. Her face filled only with love. She kissed the boy on the top of the head.

Both of them had dark, tightly curled hair. His coarser than hers. They looked as if they could be mom and son. Her heart ached at the display of love from the mom trying to soothe her child. She lifted her camera and began taking photos almost without thinking.

The boy closed his eyes, but the pain on his face remained. She zoomed in to get a closer picture. Faint lines bracketed his mouth. His lip was bruised and swollen. The woman's mouth moved, but Liv couldn't hear what was being said. The boy nodded, but his face crumpled. He turned to his mother, and she gripped him in a hug. His shoulders shook.

Liv's camera took pictures as quickly as her fingers would allow. So much love and pain against the backdrop of the serene night passed between these two. It took a second before she realized her face was wet with her own tears.

She took a deep breath and approached them. "Excuse me. I'm sorry to interrupt."

The boy jumped away from his mother. The woman straightened her shoulders. "Yes?"

"My name is Liv Scirocco. I'm a local photographer. I'm putting together an exhibit of my work. I snapped some photos of you. Could I show you?"

"You did what?" The woman backed away with confusion on her face.

"I know it sounds crazy. I work for a local insurance company that wants pictures of the car accidents. My boss sent me out to get some shots of the cars. You two caught my attention. You're so in sync with each other. I wanted to capture your love. Not your grief. Can I show you?"

The son looked at his mother and shrugged. She wiped some hair away from her face. "Okay. Sure."

She positioned the camera for them both to look at

and toggled through the photos.

"How did you do that?" the woman said.

"Do what?" She hoped she hadn't offended this woman. If some stranger had come up to her on the street, she probably would've marched away with some choice words. But in Water Course, people were different. They trusted in a way she had never learned to do completely. But she would try now if she and Hud were going to find their boy.

"Make me look like so pretty, and I don't know, full of life or something."

"That's how you look." Her insides smiled for the first time that she wasn't with Hud. "Here's my card." She dug a dog-eared card out of her wallet. "Take a look at my website. If you don't mind, I'd like to reach out to you about the exhibit."

"Of course. Here's my number." The woman gave her a cell number and took her card.

"Thanks. Good luck with the car."

She had the direction she wanted to take her career in. She couldn't wait to tell Hud her plan. If she was going to pull off the ideas swimming around in her head, she would have to eat some crow from her former life to make it happen.

If only she hadn't dumped that bowl of punch. If only she hadn't done a bunch of things, but that wasn't the case. She needed to start doing things to make her son, if he wanted to know her, proud of her.

CHAPTER 18

The phone rang somewhere in the distance. Hud wiped a hand over his face and untangled himself from Liv. Before he could finish rolling over and slapping for the phone, the ringing stopped. He must've been dreaming.

The bedroom was dark except for the sliver of moonlight slipping around the sides of the shades and drawing white lines on the walls. The hour had to be late or very early morning. His phone lit up and rang again.

"Who the hell is calling at this hour?" Liv groaned into her pillow.

"Good question." He grabbed the phone. The screen lit up and nearly blinded him. "It's Owen." He bolted upright. The fog of sleep disappeared with the racing of his heart.

"Owen?" Liv sat up too.

"Hey," he said into the phone. "Everything okay?" He threw the covers back and grabbed a pair of sweatpants. The room was cold outside of the blankets and Liv's warm body.

Liv climbed to her knees, watching him with wide eyes.

"Hey, man. Sorry to call at three in the morning, but I was so excited I couldn't wait." Owen's voice came through loud and clear.

His heart picked up speed. He took a deep breath to steady it. This was the moment they had been waiting weeks for. "I'm going to put you on speaker so Liv can hear."

"Hi, Livvie."

"Hey, Owen." She tucked her hair behind her ear.

"We found him," Owen said.

He sank onto the bed. His legs couldn't hold him with the weight of that reality. Liv pressed against his back and rested her chin on his shoulder. She sobbed.

"Tell us everything," he said.

"My friend Chase, the guy I told you about, he used that license plate number your father had written down. It was a dead end at first. But believe me when I tell you this, Chase has some crazy talents and access to resources you see in Liam Neeson movies. Anyway, it took some time, but he did it."

He couldn't breathe. He was one step closer to

seeing his son. He had promised Liv he would take this whole thing slowly, but now that their son had been found, he wanted to leave right now to get to him. Enough time had been wasted and taken from them. He wanted their new life to begin immediately.

"Where is he?" he said.

"He's in Salisbury, Pennsylvania, in Bucks County. Maybe an hour and half away from us." Owen's voice echoed in their dark room. They hadn't even bothered to turn on the light.

"Do you have his name?" Liv's breath was warm on his neck. She dug her nails into his arm, but he didn't say anything. He was her anchor, which was what he wanted to be for her.

"His name is Jay Vernon. The people who took him are Marcus and Vivian Vernon." Owen had avoided saying parents. Hud appreciated his discretion. "As far as Chase can tell, they are good people and have done a fine job of raising him. He's a normal teenager that goes to public school, and gets decent grades, Chase has his report card if you want it. Jay plays basketball on the high school team, and has no unusual health conditions."

"He got all of that?" Liv said.

"I told you he was good. What Chase doesn't know is if these people know what they did was illegal. There's a very strong chance they thought the adoption was legit. They were given a birth certificate with their names on it and paid money to an actual adoption agency. Chase has a copy of that too."

"Now what?" he said.

"That's up to you two. I'll email you the file Chase put together. If you want to show up at your son's door, you can. If you want to hire a lawyer, I'll connect you to one of mine. Even if this Marcus and Vivian Vernon don't know what they did is illegal, it still is."

"And if we don't do anything?" Liv said.

He turned to her. "What are you saying?"

Before Liv could answer, Owen jumped in. "Like I said, you two have to decide. If you need anything else, let me know."

Liv moved off the bed and went into the bathroom, shutting the door and him out. He stood to follow her, but stopped.

"What do I owe you and your friend?" he said instead.

"I told you. Nothing. This is my gift to you."

"I can't let you do that." He would pay his own way on this. This Chase guy had gone above and beyond for them because of Owen. He owed this man everything for finding his boy. For finding Jay. He swirled his son's name around in his head. It was a fine name.

"You're coming with me to clean up some beaches, man. I don't want anything else from you ever. And truth now, Chase didn't bill me for his time either. He said he'd do anything to help parents find their kids. He doesn't charge for that kind of work."

"So, he's a saint," Liv said, coming out of the bathroom.

"His wife thinks so." Owen laughed. "The email is coming now. Let me know what else I can do for you. I know you won't get any more sleep. Hope you'll forgive me for that one. Night." Owen ended the call before he could thank him again.

He switched on the lamp. Liv's hair swirled around her head in untamed curls. She was beautiful with sleep still in her eyes and wearing his t-shirt. "We did it. We can go to him. Let's leave when the sun comes up."

"What are we going to do, just show up on his doorstep? Shouldn't we have a plan or something? Maybe Owen had a good idea about a lawyer." She leaned against the dresser, keeping space between them.

"I don't want to wait for a lawyer. That could take weeks. We have a right to see our son now." He didn't understand why she was holding back. She had to be as excited as he was. He suspected she would be afraid or worried, but they had been waiting for this moment. They finally had a second chance. How many people would dream about this?

"But we have to do it the right way. Owen said he has a good life. We can't just show up and blow it open on him. We have to protect him."

"And you think sending a lawyer won't blow open his world?" At least if they showed up, it would still seem personal. A letter from a lawyer would be cold and calculated.

"But at least we'll look legitimate and serious. If we show up banging on his door with our emotions erupting, we'll look like crazy people."

"I need some coffee." He didn't want to think about what Liv had said. She had a point, but he also didn't want to wait for some suit to tell them how to handle this. He was tired of playing by the rules.

He had spent his entire adult life following the path set before him. He wanted to do things his way for once. He would never hurt his son, but he wanted to be the one to see these people's faces when they found out what had happened. He was owed that much.

Liv's footsteps followed him into the kitchen. He busied himself with grabbing a coffee pod and starting up the machine. "Do you want any coffee?"

"Hud, did you hear what I said?" Liv crossed her arms over her chest and tapped her foot.

"I'm doing this. I'm going to show up at the Vernon's house and tell them I want my son back. My fucking son." He banged the mug on the counter. She jumped.

He closed his eyes and tried to count to ten, but the fire in his veins kept his mind reeling and any chance of calm out of reach.

"Look at me." She shoved him. Tears brimmed in her eyes.

"Livvie—"

"Don't 'Livvie' me right now. I know you're hurting something fierce. I am too. I'm scared to death. But what scares me more than the idea that we know where our son is, is losing you to all of this. I can't lose you again."

"You aren't going to lose me." He didn't know how to make her understand. It was as if he tried to grab onto the sand, but it wouldn't stay in his hand.

"Really? What are you going to do if the Vernons call the cops after we tell them the story? If they do know they stole our child, do you think they'll be willing to have a sensible conversation with us? Are you going to be able to just walk away?"

"I don't know."

"Well, I do. I know you. You're still the same man I fell in love with years ago. You've got your teeth in this, and you won't let go. You are determined to make things happen. It's a great trait, but now, it could undo you. I can't watch you kill yourself trying to make our son come back to us." She swatted at the tears on her face. He didn't want to make her cry, but she was right. He was determined to see this through.

"He belongs with us." The coffee machine filled the mug, but he no longer wanted or needed the coffee. The adrenaline pumped just fine through his veins.

Liv took the coffee and poured milk in it. She eyed him over the top of the mug. She understood him in ways no one else had, and she wouldn't let him get away with his shit either.

"I want him back too, but he might not actually belong to us anymore. Don't you know how much that kills me to say that? But we have to think about him. Not Marcus and Vivian Vernon and not us."

"I have to go there and see him. I don't want to bring a lawyer in. I don't want to give them a heads-up. If they stole him, they could be likely to pack up and leave. Maybe even change their names again. I'm sorry I yelled, but I have to do this, and I don't want to do this without you. Please tell me you'll come with me."

CHAPTER 19

*L*iv stared at her hands in her lap. She couldn't move, and she couldn't undo what was about to happen. Her heart filled her throat. The roaring in her ears drowned out the car door opening.

"Sweetheart, are you ready?" Hud held his hand out. So much strength was in his grip, but once she put her hand in his, she would tumble into a black hole.

There was no going back. She had agreed to go along with Hud's idea, but the rock in her stomach said she had made a mistake. Facing Hud now and telling him no would kill him just as surely as it would kill her. But what would their presence do to the innocent boy in all of this?

"Hud, are you sure we're doing the right thing?"

"It's time. We need to catch them before Marcus leaves for work." The line of his jaw was set.

She hadn't been able to convince him to at least seek out a lawyer, but a part of her believed Hud was right too. The constant warring in her brain had drained her. She needed what strength she had left to stand before the Vernons and claim their son. She didn't want to hurt her boy, but she wanted him deep in her soul. She had wanted him from the second she had learned she was pregnant. The minute she had learned she would be a mother, she wanted a better life. On a long breath, she took Hud's hand and stepped out of the car. He was right. That boy was theirs.

He adjusted the file folder and wrapped her in his arms. "It's going to be okay."

The file that Owen had sent over also detailed the daily comings and goings of the Vernon family, including pictures of their stone-front farm house; Marcus Vernon in his suit and carrying a metal coffee mug, leaving each morning thirty minutes after Jay caught the school bus; and Vivian Vernon running errands around town.

"What if it isn't?"

"They already took Jay. It can't get any worse than that."

Jay. She still tried the name on as if she could change it for a better fit. It wasn't the name they had picked out if they were to have a boy. She had wanted to name him after Hud, but Hud had insisted they not do that. Too confusing, he had said. They had settled on Andrew because it was a strong name and would call him Drew for short. They gave that name instead to the baby they buried.

They headed up the cement front walk. The windows were outlined with black shutters and the paneled front door painted to match gleamed in the sunlight. The landscaping was simple and asleep for the winter. This could be a house in any story. It would have been easier to fight this battle if these people had been unfit in some way, but the truth was she would've been the unfit mother.

"Hey, I can hear your brain from over here. They don't make better parents than we do." Hud rang the bell.

"How can you be so sure?"

"We made him out of love." He placed a quick kiss on her lips.

No one answered the bell. Why had she agreed to this? She fought back the bile. Hud had been so determined to do it his way. She understood his point that if the Vernons did know Jay was stolen, they would run. Anyone would. But he was prepared to show up at Jay's school with the file if they refused to tell him the truth about his birth. She hoped that wouldn't have to happen.

The door swung open. "Can I help you?" A tall woman with straight gray hair to her shoulders pulled a tan cardigan closed. She had an unsuspecting smile and bright-blue eyes. The warmth from inside the house drifted out to the porch.

"Are you Vivian Vernon?" Hud said. She wasn't sure her mouth would work during any of this, and Hud had wanted to be the one to ask the questions.

"Yes. Who are you?" She put a hand on the door as if she might need to be ready to slam it shut.

"My name is Hudson Lozado and this is Liv Scirocco." He paused.

The woman stared. The names didn't seem to register with her. She either had no idea who they were or she had been rehearsing this moment for the past fifteen years.

"We were hoping to talk to you and your husband about your son Jay." Hud adjusted the file under his arm.

"Is there something wrong with Jay? Are you the police?" She clutched the collar of her sweater. "Marcus, come here." She turned inside the house and called for the husband.

A middle-aged man with sleeked gray hair and a charcoal suit came down the hallway. His dress shoes clicked against the tile. "Who's at the door? Can I help you two?" Marcus Vernon's gaze bounced between her and Hud.

"They want to talk to us about Jay. Did he go to school today?"

Marcus ignored his wife's question and addressed

them. "What about him? Did he skip school? Are you the truant officers?"

"No, sir. We're his parents." Hud squared his shoulders. She gripped his elbow to keep her shaking legs from dropping her on her ass.

"Excuse me?" Vivian spit out a creaky laugh.

"Is this some kind of joke?" Marcus said.

"No, sir. You adopted a baby from an agency in Water Course, New Jersey, fifteen years ago. A Dr. Lozado met you outside his medical practice in the late hours of the night explaining a story about the urgency of you taking the baby right away. You were given a birth certificate with your names already printed on it." Hud pulled out a copy of the birth certificate from his file. The certificate was filled out now with no proof of how it had been given to the Vernons, but Hud's dad had admitted as much.

"How do you know that?" Marcus stared at the birth certificate and handed it back.

"My father is Dr. Lozado." Hud held the man's gaze, but he slipped his hand into hers. She squeezed it to let him know she wouldn't let go.

"So?"

"My father gave you our child without our knowledge. He delivered our baby during a snowstorm and told us the baby had died during delivery. Then he arranged for you to take him the same night."

"Come inside. It's freezing out here and you're shivering." Vivian stepped back and waved them in.

Marcus glared at his wife and her invitation.

"We can't have this conversation on the front stoop, Marcus."

"But they're lying."

"We're not." She finally found her voice, and she was shaking, but it wasn't entirely from the cold. "Why would we? Why would two strangers show up at your door claiming to be the biological parents of your son if they were lying? You know you didn't give birth to him. You know you were given a newborn in an unorthodox manner. Surely, you must've thought the appearance of his biological parents was a possibility."

"Please come inside. We have nosy neighbors." Vivian ushered them inside and into a living room off the hall.

The room was cozy with a brick fireplace and bookshelves from floor to ceiling. An ornate rug covered the wide-planked hardwood floors. A photograph of them with a boy around the age of eight all sitting together on the grass with a red barn behind them hung on the wall. A family portrait taken one fall afternoon to commemorate the love and togetherness they shared. That should've been her and Hud with their boy.

"Can I get you some coffee?" Vivian said.

"No, thank you." Hud stayed in the doorway to the

room. She stood beside him, needing his strength more than ever.

"I have to call the office and let them know I'll be late. Excuse me a minute." Marcus headed down the hall toward a kitchen.

"Mr. Vernon, I would appreciate it if you didn't leave the room until we're through. I can let you borrow my phone if you'd like." Hud pulled his phone from his jacket pocket.

"What are you getting at?" Marcus narrowed his eyes.

"Oh, for goodness sakes, Marcus. They think we took their child. He's worried you're going to call someone about it."

"Took their child? Are you two crazy? Is this about money? Are you trying to exploit us?" Marcus's face took on an unhealthy red hue.

"This isn't about money. There's no point in denying the way you received a baby was less than orthodox. Everyone standing in this room knows what happened that night. The question is, does Jay?" Hud said.

"Did you take him?" Her voice trembled. Now that they were standing in their home, she wanted to know it all. Every detail of the moment they came and carried her baby away.

Marcus paced the small space. His shoes made

muffled sounds on the carpet, then more tapping as he hit the hardwood.

"I'll admit the way we adopted Jay did seem strange, but the doctor, I guess your father, and the man from the agency assured us everything was fine. They claimed the young mother was in a hurry to have the baby given to the adoptive parents, afraid she might change her mind." Marcus loosened his tie.

"Is that why you used a fake name when you met my father?"

"How did you know about that?" Vivian dropped to the antique style sofa.

"We know everything." Hud held up the folder. "It's all in here, and my father told me the rest."

"The agency said it would be better if the doctor didn't know who we were and accidently tell the mother. They were concerned she would search us on the internet. We feared for years she would show up, but when that never happened, we figured the agency was being overly cautious." Marcus stopped the incessant back and forth.

"We were told it was a closed adoption." Vivian pulled the cardigan closed again.

"It didn't seem weird to you to take a baby in the middle of the night?" Hud said.

"It did. I questioned it, but the agency said it was unusual for a teenage mother to want an older couple for the adoptive parents. He had implied that she had to be convinced to choose us," Marcus said.

"I was desperate for a child. We had tried for such a long time to have one of our own, but I had too many medical problems. When the agency called with a baby, we saw that opportunity as a gift. We didn't question it. Well, I certainly didn't." Vivian stood again and stepped beside her husband.

"You should have asked a lot of questions because our child was taken from us, and we want him back." Hud's eyes turned to black ice. The anger vibrated off him in waves.

They weren't supposed to tell them they wanted their son back so soon. They were going to explain what had happened to them. How they had been the victims, and they needed the Vernons' help. They were supposed to tell them about Hud's medical condition first.

Vivian gasped.

"What proof do you have that our boy was yours? We adopted him from a legitimate agency. I paid thousands of dollars. You can't come in here and demand our son is yours. And even if he is, you gave him up for adoption. You don't get to have him back like a borrowed library book."

She gripped Hud's arm to focus on something other than the tears threatening to choke her. "Mr. and Mrs. Vernon, we didn't give up our son. We were told he died during the delivery. I had been sedated, and Hudson was stuck in a snowstorm trying to get to me. His father took the baby and gave him to you. We never wanted to get rid of our child."

"I don't believe you," Marcus said. "This is about money. You're trying to blackmail us."

"We don't want your money." Hud handed over the folder. "Here's our proof that your adoption wasn't on the up and up. It's enough for us to hire a lawyer and come after you for kidnapping. My father has admitted to me that he lied about the death of our son. I can have him subpoenaed if this goes to court. We can also have the body of the child we buried exhumed and a DNA test done. We're certain a DNA test performed on Jay would show he's ours."

Vivian began to silently cry. Marcus grabbed the folder, but dropped it on a marble-topped table as if it burned his hand. She wished it had.

"What do you want?" Vivian's voice was barely above a whisper.

"We want our son back. I can't make that any simpler for you," Hud said.

"Does he know he's adopted?" No matter what happened, she didn't want to ruin Jay's life. The Vernons seemed like decent people. They might even be telling the truth about their part in the adoption. If Jay was happy, then it might be better if he stayed. She didn't know how to convince Hud of this. He wanted his son back, and she understood that too.

"Yes, of course," Vivian said. "We told him it was a closed adoption with no information on the biological parents. He used to ask us about locating his birth parents, but he's stopped over the past few years. Without any information, he doesn't know where to look."

"What's he like?" She wanted to understand him. Get a better idea of what his world consisted of. She wanted to ask the questions they had planned on before telling these people what they were after.

"He's very serious. He thinks everything through before acting, but he's so determined to accomplish whatever he puts his mind to. He has drive in spades." Vivian's face lit up as she spoke of her son.

But her heart crushed against her ribs. This woman had described Hud. She glanced at him. His face was covered in pain as if he wore a mask. His lips were drained of color. His mouth was bracketed with deep lines. Even the circles under his eyes had returned. She wondered if he felt okay or needed to sit, but she couldn't ask in front of the Vernons. It would kill him if she did.

"You can't take him from us," Marcus said.

"Why? Because it would be wrong to steal your child?" Hud's words cut through the room.

"We didn't know. You have to believe us. I had

desperately wanted to be a mother. I could never have taken a child from another woman."

"Here's the deal," Hud began. "We're staying at a bed and breakfast in town for the night. You have until tomorrow after school to tell Jay the truth or we will. We know where the school is, and we'll wait for him. Don't try to take him and run. I already have someone working on ways to track you if you try."

He had spoken to Owen and Owen's friend Chase the day before. Chase had helped them form the plan and was already watching the house in case the Vernons did try to leave with Jay. She had left the details to Hud and the other guys. She only wanted to witness, not orchestrate. She was torn in too many pieces like an unwanted photograph.

"You'll upset him if you just spring the truth on him," Vivian said.

"We'll take the chance because we believe he should know the truth. We also believe you knew what you were doing when you took him. If I were you, I'd tell him about that night, not just that his biological parents showed up." Hud shifted his weight from one foot to the other. He must be hurting. She wanted to leave and go back to the bed and breakfast and give him a chance to simmer down.

"We need more time," Marcus said. "Jay has a basketball game tonight. He won't be home until late."

"You aren't getting any more time. You've had

fifteen years to tell him the truth." Hud lunged forward and pointed a finger in Marcus's face.

"We didn't steal him." Marcus's face turned an even brighter red. A vein bulged on the side of his neck. "You have to believe us. We aren't criminals. Let me get the papers. I'll show you. I don't know what happened to you, but we adopted a boy. He's our son. We love him. He's our whole world. You can't rip that world apart."

"I'm afraid it's too late for that because our world was ripped apart too. Come on, Liv, let's go." Hud ushered her out of the house.

She drank in the cold air. Her lungs could finally expand. She went to the car on quivering legs, but she managed to slip inside beside Hud. He pulled away without a word or a look back. When they went around the corner, he pulled over and parked. He rested his head on the steering wheel.

"Are you okay? Do you feel sick?" She placed a hand on his shoulder. She couldn't lose him now.

"My physical heart is fine." He didn't move. She wondered if he was telling the truth.

"You looked so upset in there. I was worried you might collapse."

He turned to her. "How are you staying so calm?"

"I'm not. Believe me. The whole time I thought I might be sick right in that pretty room. But I keep thinking about Jay and what's best for him."

"I was so angry standing in that house. They had our life with our kid. And to sit there and accuse us of getting the adoption wrong. They pretended like they were victims too. How could they?"

"In some ways, they are. If they truly believed they were adopting from a legitimate agency, us showing up at their door would be a shock. Let's go back to the room and just close the curtains, order in, and try and relax. I can't take the stress anymore, and you shouldn't either." They hadn't told the Vernons about Hud's heart condition. They would have to before they left.

"I want to go to that basketball game today."

"I don't know if that's a good idea." She wanted to get out of the car. The sun heated up the inside and made her sweat. She needed space and fresh air or she might lose her mind.

"We can hide in the back. I promise, we won't say anything to anyone. I just want to see him play. Please, Liv. I might not get another chance." The pleading in his voice shook her. She had hurt him enough in this lifetime. The least she could do was give him this.

Hud had played in high school too. He was good at it like everything else he did. He could've played in college, but his father discouraged him by saying basketball wouldn't give him a career he could rely on. For him to have a son who played too would've been a dream come true for him.

"Okay." She didn't know how to say no to him, and

she didn't know if seeing their son would destroy him. "Can we go to the bed and breakfast until then?"

"Sure. Thanks for understanding on this one." He pulled the car back out onto the road.

They didn't say anything else until they were in the room. The bed and breakfast was tucked into the small town like a nesting toy. The view from their room was of the street, but she closed the curtains as soon as they returned. The bright day with its clear blue sky was far too cheery for her.

"Are you hungry? I can get us some lunch." Hud glanced at a menu for a café down the road.

"I don't think I can eat. I'm going to take a nap." She kicked off her shoes and climbed onto the floral comforter. The bed cocooned her in its soft mattress. She wanted to close her eyes and forget for a little while.

"Liv, this is going to all work out. You'll see. We're going to get our boy back."

"I don't want to talk about it right now."

The bed shifted under his weight. He ran his hand over her hair. She opened one eye. He smiled at her. "Are you mad at me?"

"No, I understand what's going on with you. But I'm not sure if you have Jay's best interests at heart because you have your mind made up, and I don't want to keep him from you either. You deserve to have him back."

"You don't want him?"

"Of course, I do." She sat up and faced him. "I've wanted him back every single day. It took me months, years, before I could go a whole day without thinking about him. But I'm scared. I'm so scared I'm going to do the wrong thing. I've already screwed up so much. What makes me think I'm doing the right thing now?"

"I'm sorry. I am going too fast, and I promised I would take things slowly, like I usually do." He gave her his impish grin and shrugged. "We'll go to the game later today, then we'll wait to hear from the Vernons. No more talk about the future. Take a nap. I'll get us some lunch." He kissed her and left the room.

She stared at the ceiling. The minutes ticked away. Sleep never came, and Hud didn't return.

CHAPTER 20

$\mathcal{H}$ud walked every street in the small Pennsylvania town with stores lining the sidewalks and churches that had been converted to restaurants. The river was on his right and blowing a stiff wind into him. He dug his hands into his pockets and hunkered down in his coat, but that did little to keep him warm. He bumped into a few people along the way because his eyes might be open, but he couldn't focus.

He had been only feet from where his son slept each night, and he couldn't go near his room and see what was on his walls or what lined his dresser. Did he have a computer on a desk? Did he like to read? He had stood in the same place as Jay had and couldn't feel his presence. *Jay.* His son.

His feet slapped against the sidewalk as he made his

way back to the bed and breakfast. He had promised to bring Liv lunch, but he hadn't stopped anywhere. Every time he had started to order something, he couldn't. He couldn't keep his mind off the way the Vernons had looked at him as if he had lost his mind. He hoped he had made his point with them. Nothing would stop him from telling Jay the truth.

Liv had texted him three times. He hadn't responded. He was being an ass. She didn't deserve that, but he wasn't ready to talk. He didn't want to hurt her, so he would make it up to her for what he was doing.

It was almost time to go to the basketball game. He ducked inside a deli and ordered turkey sandwiches then hurried back to Liv, ready to take whatever she gave him for his disappearance this afternoon.

He opened the door to their room. She swung around at the sound of the creaking hinges and glared at him. He wanted to hang his head. "I'm sorry."

"Where have you been? I've been worried something happened to you or that you decided to go back to the Vernons and beat the information out of Marcus." She crossed the room in two strides and poked her finger in his chest.

"I was walking." He put the food down on the desk in the corner and shrugged out of his jacket.

"Walking where? And why didn't you answer my texts?" She fisted her hands on her hips.

"I should have." He took the sandwiches from the bag and opened the bottled water.

"Yes, you should have. What's going on with you?" The anger drained some from her voice.

"I don't know. I felt stuck or something. I needed air then I needed to keep moving. Every step made me want to walk more and the more I walked the worse I felt." He couldn't explain it, not the way she could anyway. He was conflicted too about Jay and what was right for him, but the ache deep in his gut told him to fight for his son. To fight for his son in a way his father had never fought for him.

"So, why didn't you come back here to me?"

"I'm here now."

"Oh no, you don't get to dismiss this or me. We made a deal to get through this together. You asked me not to leave you during this ordeal of claiming our son. The same goes for you. I can't handle this by myself. I'm not strong enough to do this alone." Her voice broke. She marched over to the window and turned her back to him.

"I'm sorry. I won't leave you." He gripped her shoulders, but she didn't move. "I just needed some space. I should've sent you a text to tell you I was okay. It won't happen again."

She turned in his grip. "You're damn right it won't happen again. You listen to me, Hudson Lozado. I don't care if you need space or a trip to Hawaii with your friend to play on the beach, but you will not shut me out. Ever. We're through if that happens again."

He bit the inside of his cheek to keep from smiling at her because that would piss her off more. She was beautiful when she got fired up. He loved her for standing up to the whole world even when that meant standing up to him.

"I promise. I'll tell you what's going on with me always."

"Always. That word defines us."

He didn't want to talk. He wanted to hold her and love her. He cupped her face and brought his lips to hers. She tasted sweet and minty. She rewarded him by opening her mouth to his and tangling up their tongues. He let all the other thoughts crowding his mind disappear as the kiss deepened and she moaned against his mouth. That sound sent all his blood south.

She slipped her hands up his shirt and set his soul on fire. Each time with her the urgency to touch and taste and feel threatened to burn him alive. He wanted all of her at once. At first, he was afraid she wouldn't like his desperation, but she matched him with an unquenchable need to be naked and making love.

She undid his belt and shoved his pants over his hips. He hiked her onto the little table in the corner. She shimmied out of her jeans and gripped him. He didn't wait. Couldn't wait. He was inside her, thrusting. Her heat surrounded him and made his head spin.

He gripped her butt and pulled her closer so he could completely fill her up. She cried out his name and clawed at his back. He dropped his mouth to her neck and bit down as his climax hit him hard and fast. Their bodies trembled, slick with sweat as his heart found its natural rhythm again.

"Holy shit." She ran her tongue up his neck and nibbled on his earlobe.

"I'm sorry that was so fast. I can't seem to control myself around you." He held her close.

"I liked it. I like the way sometimes you take your time when we're together, showing me how you feel, and I also like what just happened because you so rarely lose control." She placed soft kisses on his shoulder.

He tilted her chin to force her gaze up. "Liv, I really am sorry about today. I wasn't trying to use sex to distract you from what I did."

"Apology accepted for blowing me off. Let's forget it, okay?" She eased out of his embrace and adjusted her clothing.

"You were wrong about something." He did the same and buckled his belt.

"What's that?" She narrowed her eyes.

"You are stronger than you know."

"I hope you're right because except for the past ten minutes, all I've wanted today is to have a drink." She unwrapped the white paper around the sandwich and handed it to him.

"But you didn't." He was so proud of the way she was handling all of this. She was doing a much better job than he was. She would always be his guiding light bringing him home.

"What if I do start drinking some day? I mean, I don't want to, I will do everything in my power to make sure it doesn't happen, even go to those meetings with Hawk smirking at me the whole time, but what if I screw up?"

"Then we'll deal with it together." Because he would not live one minute without her. He didn't care about her demons. He had his own.

"Like we're dealing with this mess we've gotten ourselves into." She took a bite of her sandwich.

"Exactly." He did the same.

"Well, fuck."

In spite of it all, he laughed.

THE GYMNASIUM of the high school smelled like sweat and popcorn. Liv wrinkled her nose as she and Hud climbed to the top of the bleachers and sat in the corner away from the crowd of parents and students already cheering for the home team.

The game had begun a few minutes ago. They had agreed to wait to enter until most of the crowd was already inside. They didn't want to risk seeing the Vernons, should they be there to root Jay on. They also didn't want anyone to accidently put together the resemblance between Hud and Jay. From the pictures at the Vernons' house, Jay looked as if Hud had spit him out.

She searched the court for Jay. Her breath caught when she found him passing the ball. His last name on the back of his jersey was the giveaway, but she would've recognized him without it. He was Hud at that age.

"He looks just like you." She whispered in his ear so no one around them could accidently hear.

Hud gave a thin smile and squeezed her hand. He hadn't let go of her since they got out of the car. She didn't mind. She needed to feel him for fear he would disappear before her eyes.

They sat in the bleachers watching the game until the end. Jay's team won by eight points. Many of which he had scored. Jay was a natural on the court. The way she had expected him to be. She wondered if he were even a little like her and hoped he was in some way.

The crowd cheered. A girl in a cheerleading uniform ran to Jay at the end of the game. He lifted her up and twirled her around. She planted a kiss on his lips.

"That must be his girl." The smile on Hud's face could light up the gymnasium.

Jay's teammates high-fived him for his excellent playing. Some kids from the stands came onto the floor to speak, laugh, and joke with him. The crowd thinned out, but they stayed seated. Marcus and Vivian stood off to the side of the court, waiting for a chance to get in on the action around their...around Jay. Jay saw them and went over, leaving his crowd of friends. He shook hands with Marcus and hugged Vivian who wiped at her eyes.

She stole a glance at Hud. Tears were in his eyes, but the vibrant smile remained. The truth was right before her. All she had to do was grab hold of it. And not let it slip through her fingers.

CHAPTER 21

*H*ud made his way out of the gym and to the parking lot. Liv walked beside him without saying anything. He could guess what she thought. That he was being a stubborn ass who couldn't think about anything except his own needs.

His heart filled with pride for Jay. His boy had a talent on the court. He seemed to be well liked and a good student. Marcus and Vivian seemed to be good parents who loved their child. Jay wasn't in any harm with these people. He and Liv couldn't have done any better raising him.

The cold air smacked him in the face and cleared his head. Cars made their way out of the lot in a slow crawl. Marcus and Vivian were up ahead about to get in their car.

He grabbed Liv's hand and pulled her aside. "I don't

want to take him away from his parents and his life. He belongs here." The tears, he fought, choked him from saying any more.

She put a cool hand on his face. "Are you sure?"

He nodded, afraid to speak and change his mind. Leaving Jay with the Vernons was the right thing to do. Liv was right about that. What kind of a father would he be if he allowed his son to be hurt by his hand? He could never be like his father. His father had destroyed him by taking his son away. He would not repeat history.

"Oh, Hud, I know how hard this is for you."

"It hurts worse than the heart attack did." His bit his trembling lip.

"It's okay to cry." Tears ran down her face.

He couldn't fight it anymore. He hadn't shed one single tear since the night he believed his son had died. He had been taught that real men didn't cry, but now he knew that wasn't true because the tears spilled freely down his face, burning a path that would change him forever. And nothing had been more real or made him more of a grown-up than knowing he could never have a life with his son.

"Let's flag down the Vernons before they leave." He wiped his face and stepped into the path of their car.

Marcus scowled from behind the wheel. Vivian's eyes grew wide. He hoped his lips were in a smile. He wanted them to know he meant peace.

Marcus jumped out of the car. "What are you doing here? Has he seen you?" His gaze searched the lot like a rabid animal. Vivian came around the car and joined them.

Hud put up a hand. "He doesn't know we're here. We watched him play. That's all."

"He's very good," Liv said.

"We know that. What do you want?" Marcus fisted his hands and took a fighting stance.

He wanted to assure this man he wasn't here to fight anymore and swallowed the knot in his throat. "We don't want to take him from you. He belongs here. We won't bother you anymore."

"I don't understand," Vivian said.

"Mrs. Vernon, if you can believe me, we love Jay too. I loved him from the second I knew I was pregnant with Hud's child." Liv gripped his arm and smiled up at him. "He's the best man you will ever meet and would've been an excellent father. Because of that, because we love Jay too, we want him to be happy. Happy with you two and the life you built for him." She wiped the tears from her face.

His chest hurt with the amount of love he had for her. She was braver than he ever could've been. She had known all along that Jay belonged with his parents even though it had to be tearing her up to let him go. And she had allowed him to figure it out on his own. If he had wanted to fight for Jay till the death, she had been prepared to stand beside him.

"There's one more thing more you should know," he said.

"What's that?" The scowl remained on Marcus's face. He couldn't entirely blame the guy. He would be the same way.

"I was recently diagnosed with thrombophilia. It's genetic. You should have Jay checked out for it."

"I'm so sorry," Vivian said.

"It's treatable with medicine. But I had a heart attack at work. I never saw it coming. It's better if Jay knows. Thank you for taking the time to listen to us. I'm sorry I was so difficult earlier today. Let's go, Liv."

They turned to leave.

"Wait." Vivian rummaged through her purse. "Here. Take this. So you have something of him." She gave Liv a picture of Jay. The kind of picture they take at school with the blue background. The picture shook in her hand.

He leaned over to get a better look. Jay wore a red shirt and a large smile filled with all the possibilities and arrogance a teenager could have. If he didn't know better, he'd swear he was having another heart attack the way his heart hammered around in his chest.

"He looks like both of you," Vivian said with a smile for the first time.

"Exactly like Hud." Liv beamed at him again. "The

way I always hoped he would. Thank you for this. We'll cherish it."

Liv slipped her hand into his as they made their way to the car.

"I'm proud of you," she said.

He kissed her and drove her home.

CHAPTER 22

The days stretched out with the sun coming over the horizon earlier and earlier. January was behind them now, and February promised more than longer days. Liv stood at the window of Mack's little bungalow with a mug of coffee and watched the ocean's wave spray above the jetties in small white balls of foam. She had taken to walking the beach most days and looked forward to the quiet breathing space the surf brought her. She wasn't looking forward to sharing the beach with the tourists who would arrive in a few short months.

The house wouldn't be Mack's much longer. She and Hud had made an offer to buy it. Mack and Phoenix had agreed and took Phoenix's house off the market for Mack, Phoenix and the boys to stay in.

She hadn't been sure Hud would want to remain in

Water Course, but he liked his hometown and wouldn't allow his father to run him out of it. He also understood she wanted to be near her family for now.

She checked the time on her phone. Hud would be back soon. He had been surfing each morning and getting better every day. She should move away from the window before he saw her. He accused her of watching like a nosy old hen. He promised he wouldn't have any more heart attacks. That was a promise no one could keep. Seeing him returning and turn the corner onto their street each day brought her peace. She and Hud were building a new life together. She clung to that like a light cutting through the darkness to guide her to safety.

She forced herself away from the window to wake up her computer and check emails. She was in the beginning stages of an art show with her photographs and plenty of planning was needed. The emails she enjoyed the most were from the people she photographed who thanked her for capturing the small moments in life that had meant so much to them even in the face of challenges.

The front door opened and the cold air dashed in with Hud on its heels. "Hey." He stamped his feet. The brisk weather had colored his cheeks with a dash of red. He slid off his knit cap and scratched at his hair. Her heart swelled.

"Hey, yourself. How were the waves?"

"Good. I'm going to change real quick. You hungry? I'll make some breakfast." He kissed the top of her head and ran down the hall to get out of his wet suit.

This had become their routine, and she craved it. She wasn't sure what she would do when he went to Hawaii with Owen in a few weeks. Maybe Mack would let her work at the bakery in the mornings, even for free. Too much unoccupied time gave her brain permission to think about Jay. She allowed herself five minutes a day only to wander in that direction. Her sobriety depended on the short visits.

The doorbell rang. Hud poked his head around the doorway. "Are you expecting a package?"

"Not me. I'll get it." She opened the door and nearly fell over. "Dr. Lozado, what are you doing here?"

"Hello, Olivia. Is it possible to speak to Hudson, please?" Dr. L wore a tweed flat-hat, a camel-colored parka, and a look of guilt on his face. She hadn't seen him in person since the day they buried a baby all those years ago. Time had not made facing him any easier, but at least now she had right on her side.

"What do you want, Dad?" Hud yanked his shirt over his head and stood beside her. His heat rolled off him.

"I'll leave you two alone." She tried to duck past Hud.

"No. You stay. He can leave."

She stayed, but she wanted to run in the other room.

"I won't take much of your time. I wanted to tell you that the sale of the house is finally complete. We had a few obstacles at the last minute that had delayed the closing, but that's all been settled now. I'm returning to Florida today."

"Great. Have a nice trip." Hud began to shut the door.

Dr. L put a hand up. "I'm going to put the profits of that sale into an account for you."

"I don't want your money."

Dr. L shrugged and pulled a tissue out of his pocket. He wiped his nose. "I'll put the account in Olivia's name then."

"Please don't do that." The last thing she wanted was to come between Hud and his dad. Hud was not ready to forgive his father, and she wasn't going to rush him to get there if he ever did. She also didn't want anything from the man who had stolen everything from her. If it hadn't been for a heart attack and a bowl of punch, she wouldn't even have Hud back.

"I have no other way to make amends for my decisions." He wiped his nose again.

"Is that your apology?" Hud shook his head and choked out a laugh.

"I did what I thought was best at the time." His voice was flat and void of emotion.

"Why the change of heart now?" Hud said.

His father shrugged and shoved the tissue in his jacket pocket. "We all have regrets. Even you. My lawyer will be in touch. Thank you for your time." He ambled down the walk like a worn-out old man.

"I could send you to jail for kidnapping," Hud called after him.

"But you won't," Dr. Lozado said over his shoulder.

Hud closed the door and punched it. "I'm not taking his money."

"Babe, you have to feel sorry for him." She slipped her arms around his waist and pressed against him. The scent of salt water clung to his shirt.

"Why should I?" He held her close.

"Because he's a lonely old man with nothing and no one in his life. And you, Hudson Lozado, are the exact opposite."

"Thank you for that." He kissed her long and deep. Her body responded to him like a flower to the sun.

She had been trying to find the right time to tell him her news. She had wanted it to be perfect because he deserved that, her man with so much love to give. Now would help heal some of the hurt he'd been suffering. Well, as soon as they were done kissing.

A horn honked as if someone had laid on it. She broke their embrace.

"Who is interrupting my attempt to get laid?" He winked.

"Do you think that's your dad?"

"I hope not." Hud threw open the door.

Dr. L was nowhere in sight. Instead, Blair limped up the front walk as if each step caused her pain as she dragged a rolling suitcase behind her. A car sped off down the road with the driver shaking his fist in the air.

Blair's hair hung limp as if she hadn't washed it recently. Her left eye was swollen shut. She had bruises all over her face and stitches by her lip.

"Blair, oh my God, what happened?" She reached for her sister, but hesitated in case she could break her.

"Can I stay with you? Mack said you lived here now. Just for a few days?"

"Of course, you can. Come in." She helped Blair to the couch and undid the buttons on her coat. She didn't have to ask Hud if he was okay with Blair staying. He would be, and if for some weird reason he wasn't, he would get over it.

"Can we get you anything?" Hud said.

"Hey, Hud. Thanks for letting me crash. I'm fine, really. I just need to rest." Blair smiled, then winced.

"What happened?" She helped Blair out of her coat.

"I'll tell you both later. If that's okay? You know now that I think about it, maybe some ibuprofen would be great."

"I'll get it." Hud ran down the hall toward the bathroom.

"I can't believe you're here. We were so worried about you. You weren't answering your calls." Now she could guess why. She had so many questions, and Aria would have a ton more when she saw Blair like this.

Blair put up a hand. "Livvie, shut up for five seconds, okay? I've been traveling, and my head hurts."

"You don't want to talk about it."

"Not now. But later. I promise." Blair grabbed her hand and gave it a weak squeeze.

Hud returned with the bottle and a glass of water. Her phone vibrated in her pocket. She groaned. She should ignore it, but she was still working for Milly and would be for a while longer. She couldn't miss a chance to earn a little money or find more people to photograph. If Blair didn't want to tell her what was going on, then she'd have to answer the phone.

"I should get that." She dug out the phone.

"Yes, please do." Blair leaned her head against the couch and closed her eyes.

"Who is it?" Hud said.

"I don't know." She held the phone for him to see the unknown number.

What a strange turn of events the day had taken. When she woke up this morning, she had never expected to see Hud's dad or Blair arrive on her doorstep. She had hoped for some quiet time with Hud before the day got away from them. She put a hand to her belly. The future might be bright for once, and she had wanted to share that with him.

"Hello?" she said.

"Um, hello." A deep male voice came across the line. "Is this Liv Scirocco?"

"Yes, this is she. Who's calling?"

Hud narrowed his eyes. She held up her palm.

"This is Jay. Jay Vernon."

Dear Reader,

Thank you for reading Light Upon the Darkness. I hope you enjoyed it as much as I enjoyed writing Liv and Hud's story. Please consider leaving an honest review on Amazon or Goodreads. Reviews help authors.

If you're interested in meeting the other characters of Water Course, NJ, click here for the opportunity.

If you'd like to know about my other books also consider signing up for my newsletter at https://bit.ly/2FivWNA (and get exclusive content) or visiting my website at www.staceywilk.com

ABOUT THE AUTHOR

From an early age, Stacey Wilk told tales as a way to escape. At six she wrote short stories in composition notebooks, at twelve she wrote a novel on a typewriter, in high school biology she wrote rock star romances in her binder instead of paying attention.

But it wasn't until many years later, inspired by her children and a looming birthday, that she finally took her story-telling seriously. And published her first novel in 2013. Since then, she's gone on to publish fourteen more so women everywhere could fall in love and find an escape of their own.

She isn't done telling stories. Not by a long shot. If you want to read her emotional and gripping books about family, romance, and second chances, visit her at www.staceywilk.com

To see what she writes next, follow her Facebook group for her amazing readers – Stacey's Novel Family https://bit.ly/2FK8Lae Or join her newsletter - https://bit.ly/2A0jEFk

OTHER BOOKS BY STACEY WILK

Winter at the Shore Series

No More Darkness

Through the Darkness

The Brotherhood Protectors World

Winter's Last Chance

The Last Betrayal

Her Last Word

The Last Days of Christmas

Seduced by Denial

The Heritage River Series

A Second Chance House

The Bridge Home

The Essence of Whiskey and Tea

The Big Sky Country Series

Time Won't Erase

Stay Awhile (coming 2021)

Special Forces: Operation Alpha World

Stage Fright

The Omega Team World
Silent Water

The Gabriel Hunter Series (middle grade)
Welcome to Kata-Tartaroo
Welcome to Bibliotheca
Welcome to Skull Mountain

Made in the USA
Middletown, DE
09 February 2021